"By the way, you were wrong about me."

His eyes burned with hunger as they sizzled down the length of her. "I'd never try to coerce you into becoming something you're not—for example, docile."

"You're in no immediate danger of that," she retorted.

Kyle laughed. "I didn't think I was. I just wanted you to know where I stand."

"What the heck is so funny?" she demanded, pursing her lips. "You make me feel as if my sole purpose in life is to act as comic relief!"

He kissed her impulsively on the cheek. "You make me laugh, Meg. That's not so bad, is it?"

"That depends. Are you laughing at me, with me, or in spite of me?"

"I'm laughing because you're delightful." He reached for her hand...

Other Second Chance at Love books by *Aimée Duvall*

TOO NEAR THE SUN #56
HALFWAY THERE #67
LOVER IN BLUE #84
THE LOVING TOUCH #159
AFTER THE RAIN #179
ONE MORE TOMORROW #211
BRIEF ENCOUNTER #252

Aimée Duvall says about herself: *"I love my work, especially the research, and I love combining all the finest qualities of the people I meet to form my characters. I have almost as much fun horseback riding and watching scary movies. My husband loves me in spite of the fact that I rescue small puppies from the side of the road and arrive late for meetings. Someday I will dedicate a book to my favorite ice cream."*

Dear Reader:

Before I describe this month's books, I have exciting news. In February 1986, we will introduce a completely new cover design for SECOND CHANCE AT LOVE romances! Everyone at the Berkley Publishing Group is wildly enthusiastic about our new look—a sexy, sophisticated design that is as adult as SECOND CHANCE AT LOVE romances have always been. I'll keep you posted on this important change for SECOND CHANCE AT LOVE ...

In the meantime, this month begins with *Hearts Are Wild* (#298) by new writer Janet Gray, our first romance to star a professional gambler. Emily Farrell is outwardly cool but inwardly vulnerable. Michael Mategna is everything a hero should be—and more! Shattering Emily's calm at the poker table *and* in more private surroundings, he threatens her efforts to win enough money to pay back her father's debts ... and arouses her suspicions about his real motives in pursuing her. A touch of glamour, a hint of intrigue, and a powerful love story make *Hearts Are Wild* a sure bet for any romance lover!

In *Spring Madness* (#299), Aimée Duvall creates another classically wacky romantic comedy by pairing serious-minded radio station owner Kyle Rager with bubbly deejay Meg Randall. When an emergency forces this unlikely twosome to team up on the air, they become an instant hit, an unexpected challenge to their rival station ... and wildly attracted to each other! Nonstop action, zippy dialogue, and outrageous situations all make *Spring Madness* another rollicking roller coaster of a romance from Aimée Duvall.

In *Siren's Song* (#300), ever-popular Linda Barlow creates a powerfully romantic—and deliciously mysterious—world, where everything is not what it seems. When undercover agent Rob Hepburn invades the isolated island home of Cat MacFarlane, he wonders if Cat is really an innocent songstress ... or an accomplice to an international crime ring. Cat wonders if Rob is really an astronomer studying UFO's ... or a dangerous rogue living out an ancient Scot's feud. Unearthly prophecies, haunting melodies, and fast-paced intrigue abound in *Siren's Song*, making it a treat to be savored.

After too long a hiatus, **Katherine Granger** is back with *Man of Her Dreams* (#301), a sparkling, funny romance you're sure to love. Lively, self-reliant Jessie Dillon just can't admit that her gorgeous next-door neighbor, Jake McGuire, is the man she's been searching for all her life. Jake, thank goodness, is definitely *not* a guy to give up easily. Knocking off the competition is no problem—though the process is hilarious—but shutting Jessie up and calming her down long enough to convince her with kisses ... well, that takes some doing! Enjoy!

Employing her unerring instinct for story lines that appeal to romance readers, **Dana Daniels** has written a compelling story of unrequited love, *Unspoken Longings* (#302). Lesley Evans vows that Joel Easterwood will never know of the secret yearning for him that is tearing her apart. She hides the pain in her heart, and the pain in her hip that resulted from a car accident, with rapier-sharp retorts and a biting wit—never realizing that Joel is equally determined to break through her defenses and bring to life the sensual, giving woman within. *Unspoken Longings* is a deeply moving romance.

In *This Shining Hour* (#303), our second new writer this month, **Antonia Tyler**, does a terrific job with a challenging combination—a blind hero who's fiercely independent and a warm, giving heroine who's both sensually drawn to him *and* instinctively wants to take care of him. Kent Sawyer is every bit as virile and confident as Eden Fairchild has ever dreamed possible, and he's eager to prove his capabilities at both business ... and pleasure. This rich love story begins as a somewhat deceptively pleasant read, but it soon packs an emotional wallop!

Until next month, happy reading ...

Ellen Edwards

Ellen Edwards, Senior Editor
SECOND CHANCE AT LOVE
The Berkley Publishing Group
200 Madison Avenue
New York, NY 10016

SPRING MADNESS

AIMÉE DUVALL

SECOND CHANCE AT LOVE BOOK

SPRING MADNESS

Copyright © 1985 by Aimée Duvall

All rights reserved. No part of this publication may be reproduced or transmitted in any form or by any means, electronic or mechanical, including photocopy, recording, or any information storage and retrieval system, without permission in writing from the publisher.

Requests for permission to make copies of any part of the work should be mailed to: Permissions, Second Chance at Love, The Berkley Publishing Group, 200 Madison Avenue, New York, NY 10016.

First edition published November 1985

First printing

"Second Chance at Love" and the butterfly emblem are trademarks belonging to Jove Publications, Inc.

Printed in the United States of America

Second Chance at Love books are published by
The Berkley Publishing Group
200 Madison Avenue, New York, NY 10016

*To Hector Rodriguez
and his bride Jo Anne,
because a second chance at love
is always special*

Acknowledgments

With special thanks to the following radio professionals who were kind enough to share their time with me:

Mary Lynn Roper, Joel Hixon, Mike Langner, Susan Dean, Cynthia Upton, Charles Maldonado, Teddy Keller;

And last, but certainly not least, Beal and Bennet.

Chapter 1

MEG RANDALL gazed out the window at the desert mesa. The Magdalena Mountains could be seen in the distance, snow still covering their hazy blue crests. At least it was beautiful here, she thought. Good thing, since Cabezon, New Mexico, might become her next home. After all she had been through during the past few months, it would be poetic justice to end up in a town whose name, translated from Spanish, meant "hard-headed."

It was so quiet outside. Here she was more likely to wake up to the sound of a rooster crowing than to the familiar cacophony of traffic beneath her window. For someone born and raised in the city, being awakened by roosters was bound to be a unique experience.

Still, she'd adjust to anything if it meant getting a deejay job here at KHAY. After she'd been fired from KSUN in Phoenix, none of the larger stations she had applied to had been willing to give her a chance. And all because of one irate advertising client! It was just her luck to have angered a man with so much clout in the industry!

Feeling renewed determination, she squared her shoulders and pursed her lips. She wouldn't think about that now. Either Kyle Rager hadn't heard about the trouble, or he didn't care, because after listening to her demo tape, he had asked her to come in for an interview.

"Ms. Randall?" A deep masculine voice reverberated behind her. "I'm Kyle Rager. Sorry to keep you waiting."

She turned and stared at the devastatingly handsome man standing in the doorway. He perfectly fit her fantasy vision of a Nordic hero. Her own five-feet, ten-inch frame, which usually gave her the psychological advantage of never having to look up at anyone, failed her now. This man was at least six inches taller than she was. His powerful build and great size combined to create an impression of formidable virility.

His rich golden hair was casually styled and slightly windblown. Although he wore a sport jacket, his light blue shirt was open at the collar. His bold gaze suggested he was a man who knew his own strengths and weaknesses, and had long ago decided that the former far outweighed the latter.

He smiled, and his expression lit up with an enticing warmth. The effect was staggering.

"My name's Meg Randall," she blurted out. "Oh, but you already know that." She stared into the deep azure pools of his eyes. Was the light playing tricks or did they shimmer from jade to blue like translucent seawater?

The hope that she might attract him physically, as he did her, flashed through her brain. Instantly she felt her cheeks burn.

"Now, what's that all about?" he asked in a tone that implied he was well aware of his effect on her.

She cleared her throat, stalling for time as she tried to think of a reply.

He lifted one eyebrow. "Won't you come into my office?" He touched her shoulder briefly, a simple gesture that caused her heart to race.

Spring Madness 3

"Thank you," she replied, determined not to allow her thoughts to wander on to such dangerous territory again.

"I enjoyed your demo tape," he said.

She used all her willpower to break his mesmeric spell on her. "I'm glad."

He waved a casual invitation for her to take a seat, then continued to his desk. "You're very good." He eased himself into the giant brown swivel chair.

Meg couldn't help but notice how his gaze dropped as she sat down and crossed her long legs. She adjusted her tailored white skirt and leaned back, trying to appear calm and in control as his eyes drifted upward over the slender curve of her hips and the gentle swell of her breasts.

To her surprise, she found herself wishing she were more abundantly endowed in strategic places. Being shaped like a model had definite disadvantages, particularly when it came to pleasing men, who most often preferred opulent measurements over meager ones. Nonetheless, she noted with satisfaction, she had managed to capture some of Kyle Rager's attention.

"You'd make a perfect model," he commented. "There's something very sensual yet dignified about the way you move. Your stature gives you a commanding presence."

His voice was enticingly husky, and her skin tingled with apprehension. She felt almost as vulnerable as if she were standing naked before him. "Thanks. I'm glad you find me attractive," she said, hoping that bringing feelings like this out into the open would help diffuse the situation.

Not this time, however, she realized as he continued. "The only problem I have is that I'm not sure your style is conservative enough for our listeners." He held up a hand to halt her protest. "I checked around, and it seems you're the cause of a great deal of controversy."

That was putting it mildly. She sighed. What had made her think the attitude toward her being fired would be any different here? Clearly, if she wanted to continue her career, she'd have to win him over. "Would you like to hear my side of the story?" she asked.

"Sure. Let's have it."

"As you have undoubtedly discovered, I used to work for KSUN in Phoenix. During my program one day I was scheduled to begin running a series of advertising spots for the Stairway to Heaven Crematorium, which had adopted a promotional campaign to try to convince people between the ages of twenty-five and thirty-five to put a down payment on their own funerals. A morbid plan for the future, you might say." She paused. "Well, their ads were really hard-sell, and in very poor taste. Their Stairway Plan offered differently priced steps toward a celestial reward. For the top of the line in cremation services the person's ashes would be flown anywhere in the world—except hostile countries—and scattered over the chosen site.

"How cheery," Kyle commented.

"I had put in a particularly long shift that day," she continued. "One of the deejays had taken off work to get married, and his time slot had been divided among the rest of us jocks. I had been given instructions to run the ad four times every hour." She shook her head. "The whole idea made my skin crawl, to be honest, so when I ran the ad for the last time on my shift that night, I decided to joke with our listeners. I ad-libbed a bit, that's all."

He raised one eyebrow. "How?"

She shifted uncomfortably in her seat. "I told the audience that for the budget-minded, Stairway to Heaven Crematorium offered a super-saver step. The loved one's ashes could be fused into a decorative paperweight with a brass nameplate that was guaranteed to add a touch of class to anyone's office."

Kyle laughed. "And since Stairway to Heaven Crematoriums are scattered throughout the Southwest, and advertised heavily over the radio, you've probably been blacklisted by every major station."

Her heart beat at a frantic pace in response to the husky timbre of his laughter. "That's it in a nutshell," she admitted.

He became serious once again. "You really blew it, you know."

"I realize that," she replied, feeling a bit annoyed. If he wasn't going to hire her, the last thing she needed was a sermon. Her spirits sagged.

"That might have been your worse faux pas on the air," he added, "but from what I hear, that's scarcely the whole story."

She cringed. How much more had he managed to find out?

"Rumor has it that once, when you were running late on your show, you decided to speed up the news. Your newsman ended up sounding like Donald Duck on the air."

"Everyone understood him," she protested. "I made sure it wasn't fast enough to obscure what he was saying." But the excuse sounded lame even to her own ears. "You see, I didn't really have a choice. I had only two minutes of air time left and I had all the news to cover."

"What about the time you ran a segment on road conditions in the city? You called the mayor on the air and demanded he explain to voters why he wasn't doing more to solve the pothole problem."

"Well, at least he was forced to face the issue. A few days later road crews started showing up all over town."

"And what about the time you told your listeners that the man pressuring City Hall to remove thorny rose-bushes from city parks deserved a pie in the face? You started an epidemic of pie 'hit' jobs. Public officials and unpopular citizens were afraid to step outside their homes for fear of being attacked with flying pies. And as if that wasn't enough, months later, in December, you complained on the air that your station didn't have a Christmas tree. Before your shift ended, KSUN had received seventy-five trees."

"No harm was done," she insisted. "We took them to

hospitals and nursing homes. Lots of people benefited."

"But you've got to admit that, at best, your methods are unorthodox." He sat back in his chair and regarded her warily. "That's what worries me most."

She was about to defend herself further when the music being piped into his office stopped abruptly. The disk jockey interrupted his broadcast to read a special bulletin: "This was just handed to me," he told the listeners. "We need all our volunteer fire fighters to report to their duty stations. Smoke and flames have been spotted coming from the top floor of the apartment building between Fourth Street and Valverde Road." There was a brief pause. Then the deejay exclaimed, "Hey, wait a minute! That's where I live!"

The static sounds of dead air followed. Kyle's eyes widened. "He couldn't have..."

"He left the booth?" Meg leaned forward in disbelief.

At that instant the receptionist burst into Kyle's office. "T. J. McKay just rushed past my desk. There's no one on the air!"

Kyle's jaw dropped, but he recovered quickly. Springing to his feet, he dashed to the door, then stopped abruptly. "What the hell am I doing? I haven't run a control booth in at least ten years!" His eyes focused on Meg. "But you have. Come on!"

She dashed after him down the hall. "Does that mean I'm hired?"

"For now."

Suddenly she had an advantage that she had no intention of letting slip past her. This was the first opportunity she'd had in months. "I don't want temporary employment," she said as they entered the booth.

"Don't push your luck," he replied, handing Meg a set of headphones. He pulled up a chair next to hers and slipped on another headset.

"I'm sorry, but I *am* going to have to press the issue," she insisted. "You're broadcasting static right now. Which will it be? Do you want a topnotch deejay who'll work harder than anyone you'll ever meet, or are you going to try and handle this solo? Like I said, I'm not looking for temporary work." She met his eyes in a challenging stare.

Kyle's eyes narrowed as he studied her. "What concerns me is your past record. When you're alone in the booth, you seem to go a little crazy. I can't afford to have you ad-lib like you did at KSUN and have the advertisers I've managed to acquire leave my station like rats diving off a sinking ship."

"Fine. If you don't want me full-time, then I'll leave and you can take over yourself." Her best chance was to force him to make a quick decision. "So which will it be?" She pointed to the console. "So far you've got only dead air."

He clenched his jaw, and his left hand curled into a tight fist. "We'll do this together, *as a team,*" he stated, clearly emphasizing the words. "But you're still responsible for what you say. Remember that." His expression had grown calmer, but she knew he was deadly serious.

"You've got it, boss." She smiled, trying to hide her nervousness and lighten the mood.

She cleared her throat. Her hands were clammy with perspiration. Unfortunately, being a disk jockey gave more that ample opportunity to really make a mess of things. She didn't need the further distraction of Kyle's presence.

Yet he made her feel more vibrantly alive than she had ever thought possible. She liked a man who was confident enough to take risks, even when the odds weren't altogether in his favor. Like the daring knights of old, he was a man who could capture any woman's imagination. *Her* response to him was basic, primitive, and, unfortunately for her, dangerously exciting.

After switching on the microphone and adjusting her headset, she said, "Hi, there, ladies and gentlemen. I'm Meg Randall, your new deejay for this morning. T. J. McKay is out chasing the fire truck. Stay with me and we'll tour the skies of New Mexico's magic Land of Enchantment. Now, a selection I've chosen especially for you." She inserted a cassette tape from the program roster into the machine and turned off her mike. After adjusting the volume of music being piped into the booth, she winked at Kyle. "We're back on the air, boss."

He breathed a sigh of relief. "All the knobs are set, and the broadcast's going fine." He took off his headphones and set them on the console.

"With me in control, of course everything's fine," she replied with newfound confidence.

His face immediately grew stern again. "Don't get too cocky, Meg. I worked hard to convince the public to start tuning us in, and I have no intention of giving you free rein. I'm not foolish enough to ignore your track record. I don't need that kind of trouble."

"Fine. If I say something you don't like, feel free to jump right in." She slid one of the microphones over to him. "Here we go." As the song ended she switched on both of their headphones.

"I have with me in the booth, ladies and gentlemen, my new partner in crime." She have him an impish grin. "He insists he's here to keep me from getting out of hand. Say hello, Kyle."

He covered his face with one hand. "Don't get too attached to her, folks. This might be the shortest association in recorded history."

"You'd better be nice to me. If you make me mad, I'll pout, and that means I won't say a word."

"In which case I'll have to fire you," he shot back.

"But you'll die of loneliness here in the booth, boss. You need me. Admit it."

"I'll do no such thing."

"Now, I want to hear from you folks out there. Let's get together and convince this man that he needs me, shall we? Anyone who can think of why he should keep me as his partner is welcome to call, and we'll put you on the air."

Kyle's eyes bulged, but before he had a chance to say anything, Meg began the next song. Without looking in his direction, she nonchalantly checked the program log before her on the counter.

"Are you crazy?" he challenged as soon as the music began.

"Relax, boss. Being a good deejay means having fun. You should be more laid back." She flashed him a reassuring smile.

"What are you talking about?" he said in exasperation. "We're dealing with smalltown people, Meg. Half of these folks have known me since I was a kid. I was raised here!"

"What's that got to do with it? We're just going to get them involved in a few hijinks."

"No one's going to call. They'll go about their business and assume I've hired a lunatic to take over T.J.'s spot."

"It *was* inexcusable of him to leave, you know. I don't usually bad-mouth a fellow worker, but I've never known a professional deejay who'd do something like that."

"I lured T.J. away from a radio station in Roswell. He's a good employee. And he's my cousin."

"Oops." What an incredible talent she had for knowing precisely the wrong thing to say.

"It's a good thing you haven't applied for diplomatic work," he teased.

She started to reply when the telephone receiver light began to glow, signifying a call was coming through. "This is Meg Randall," she answered, glancing at Kyle with an I-told-you-so look.

"Are you going to put me on the air?" a woman asked.

"Just as soon as the song finishes," Meg assured her. "And here we go now." She switched the controls back to her microphone, then adjusted the telephone equipment that would transfer the woman's voice over the air. "And who do we have here?"

"My name's Wilma Simmons. I've known Kyle Rager since he was in diapers, and I've always thought he was much too serious. You're just what he needs, young lady.

Maybe you can teach him how to have a little fun."

Kyle groaned softly, then, remembering his mike was on, reached down and shut it off.

Meg grinned. "Tell me, Wilma, what did Kyle look like in diapers? Was he a cute baby?"

"He was the most precious thing! His mother and I went to a quilting bee every Friday, and I can still remember the picture she used to show of him running around their living room with no clothes on. He had the biggest blue eyes and long golden hair. Cutest baby you ever saw!"

Meg laughed, and Kyle shot her a venomous look. As she chatted with their listener, she scribbled a fast note to him:

Don't get angry. Listeners are getting involved. They love this. We're going to be hot!

He switched his microphone on again. "Wilma, enough!" he said in a congenial voice. "You're embarrassing me in front of the most beautiful woman I've seen in years."

He scrawled a note back to Meg:

You're making me look ridiculous.

Had he really taken offense? She didn't know, but she wasn't prepared to lose this job over something so trivial. Maybe she'd better take things a little easier, she decided when the next caller phoned in.

"Kyle, this is Fred Taubes." The masculine voice echoed over the speakers. "What's this about a beautiful new lady deejay? Describe her to me!"

"Describe her to you? You're the town's playboy, Fred," Kyle said with a laugh. "As far as you're concerned, good buddy, she's two-feet-ten and weighs three hundred and twenty pounds. Her facial features are perfect, too—if you don't mind the hook nose and one eye in the middle of her forehead."

Spring Madness

"I protest!" Meg piped up.

"Play a song, Meg," Kyle intoned.

"You've got it, boss, but I owe you one."

As the tune went over the air, Kyle laughed. "I'd say we're even." His smile erased his expression of stern control, softening his features and making him look infinitely appealing.

Averting her eyes, Meg found herself staring at the triangular opening at his collar, where thick golden chest hair emphasized his masculinity. A delightfully wicked feeling coursed through her as she pictured him stripped to the waist, crushing her to him. Her fingertips tingled as she wondered what it would be like to caress his powerful torso. In her fantasy, she could almost hear him moan her name softly over and over again as she kissed his hard, muscular flesh.

All at once she realized that the real Kyle Rager was staring at her. Trying to cover up in case she had accidentally given herself away, she asked, "Who's the Fred who called on the air?"

"He's the town's Casanova."

"Did you get his number? I want to call him," she shot back good-naturedly.

"Don't call him; he's all talk. I, on the other hand, am the real thing, and I'm right here. You'll have much more fun if you stick with me." His eyes shone with devilish merriment.

She laughed, delighted that he finally seemed to be feeling at ease with her. "I'm getting all sorts of intriguing offers this afternoon," she said. "It must be my lucky day."

When the record ended, they played a taped promotion, then put their next caller on the air. "Just how ugly is this new, hooked-nosed gal of yours, Kyle?" asked a male listener.

Meg started to protest that she wasn't Kyle's gal at all, then stopped abruptly. The audience was playing along!

The shift ended two hours later. Kyle looked exhausted as he hung his headphones on the hook near the console.

Meg watched as he exchanged a few words with the disk jockey in charge of the afternoon slot. Working with Kyle today had been fun. The heightened sense of excitement that came from being near him, yet never knowing what was going to happen next, had been the key ingredient of an unforgettable morning.

But could she really work side by side with him every single day? The attraction between them was dangerous for lots of reasons. What if he made her so nervous that she ended up doing something crazy on the air? He'd probably fire her.

What to do? She couldn't very well admit the problem to him. Besides, she really did need the job.

She walked out to the hall, where Kyle joined her seconds later. Her heart froze as she saw the stern expression on his face. All traces of the congenial deejay she had shared the booth with were gone. Had he just been pretending to have fun on the air?

"What's up?" she asked, feeling as if her stomach had fallen to the floor.

"We need to talk. I'm not sure where we're heading with this partnership of ours."

"Well, now that you know I can handle the needs of your listeners, why don't you give me my own time slot? I don't care if it's the midnight shift; I'll take whatever's available."

"I'll have to think about it. Originally I planned to keep you out of trouble by staying in the booth, but, lady, you're a handful!" He ran his fingers through a lock of hair that dangled roguishly over his forehead. "Sparring with you can inflict mortal wounds. There were times this afternoon when I wondered if I would have to slip out of town unnoticed."

"I thought it went well," she insisted. "If you're worried about being uncomfortable, I promise never to say another word about you on the air again."

He stood silently, lost in thought. His eyes left a burning trail as they lingered over her in an almost sensual caress. "You're good, but you're too impulsive. I'm just not sure what to do with you. You blurt things out before considering the consequences."

She had to admit it was well-deserved criticism. "But that's what makes a deejay appealing to the listeners," she countered. "If I censor everything I say, I'll sound unnatural and too... well, too programmed."

He was about to reply when the receptionist rushed up to them. "Kyle, the station's lines have been ringing off the hook! Everyone wants to know the same thing— are you and Meg going to stay on T.J.'s time slot? They *loved* you!"

"Now I've really got problems," Kyle muttered, shaking his head.

Chapter 2

TWO HOURS LATER Meg sat in Kyle's office, once again waiting for him to get off the telephone. The response to their impromptu twosome was significant, and completely unexpected. The station's lines continued to be tied up with callers.

Kyle replaced the receiver and stared across his desk at Meg. "I never expected this reaction from the folks out there," he mused.

"Neither did I," she admitted. "I want to stay and continue working as a deejay, but I want to work solo even more. Because of the circumstances I went along with your demand to stay in the booth and maintain control of the show today, but as far as making it permanent..." She paused and shook her head. "I don't think that would be a good idea."

As it was, she was having enough trouble controlling her wildly misbehaving imagination. To work beside him day in and day out was bound to be akin to playing with matches near a gasoline pump.

15

"I'll be honest with you, Meg. Personally, I wouldn't mind sharing a close, confined sound booth with you," he teased. "But"—he grew serious again—"your exuberance on the air really worries me. Unchecked, it could create lots of problems for this station."

"Are you kidding? I was a hit! Look at all the calls," she replied, pretending not to have heard the first part of his statement. This was no time to allow him to divert her attention.

"Precisely. What they enjoyed was the way *we* interacted. Most of these people know me as a very conservative, private person. Suddenly, instead of the country music programming they were expecting, they heard you and me bantering. To find me paired with a woman who's continually going off on one wild tangent or another— well, I think they must have gone into shock." He sighed. "The truly amazing thing is that we were a hit."

She remained silent for several moments. "So, in effect, are you saying we should keep things the way they are and not argue with success?"

"Actually I'm not sure we're compatible enough to continue as a team."

"So where does that leave me?" For the second time that day she felt her hands grow clammy. She needed this job desperately, and because of that she was completely at his mercy. Surely fate wouldn't be cruel enough to make her think she had found employment, then take it away from her a short time later!

"I promised you a job," he said quietly, as if trying to sort out his thoughts.

"You certainly did," she replied, hoping he'd honor his word.

"The real question is whether or not I can allow an opportunity like this to slip by me."

Meg's pulse quickened as she met his ocean-blue eyes, which shimmered with compelling intensity. A streak of sunlight filtering through the window played on his hair, making it shine like burnished gold, and his chiseled jaw was set with the immovability of roughly hewn granite.

There was a quiet strength about him that drew her with irresistible force.

But more than his looks were creating a problem for her. The essence of him as a man insinuated itself past her defenses, confusing her with a yearning she had hoped never to feel again.

Kyle leaned back in his chair and folded his hands behind his head. "I've been having trouble finding enough sponsors to make this station run in the black. A show that receives such a favorable response is a good selling point when I try to convince businessmen to book advertising time on our station."

"Give me a chance to work with your listeners on a program of my own for a few weeks," she pleaded. "If I don't catch on, then we can try the alternative."

"It would be foolish for me to discard a popular format for an untried one. If we ignore the public's reaction to our show, we'll be wasting a golden opportunity." He pursed his lips. "I promised you a job and you'll have one—but only with me as your partner."

Men! Without thinking, she curled up her nose in protest.

"Making faces at me won't help," he said with a chuckle.

She smiled sheepishly. How could getting this job have become so complicated? To make matters worse, Kyle Rager didn't seem the type to back down once he had made up his mind. It would be his way or nothing. In that respect he reminded Meg of her ex-husband, Mike. Was she about to get involved with another domineering man who insisted on having his own way in everything? If so, her experience at KHAY was apt to be disastrous— even if it was strictly business.

She needed to exercise a bit of diplomacy, an art that was certainly not her strong suit. Even if he was the boss, she had to make sure she maintained at least partial control over the show's format. If he insisted on implementing only his own ideas, without presenting her with options, she probably wouldn't be able to function properly at her job. She'd never been any good at trying to adapt her style to someone else's. And she certainly couldn't afford to be fired from *two* jobs!

"What worries you so much about being a team?" he asked softly, in a way that weakened her defenses.

"You and I are so different," she said candidly. "I'm not sure if, in the long run, we wouldn't be courting disaster by trying to work together."

Why had she been so frank? With this admission she might have sabotaged her job at KHAY. Determined not to betray her nervousness, she forced herself not to fidget.

"Courting disaster?" he repeated. "In what way?"

His voice glided over her like a gentle summer breeze. She swallowed to rid her throat of dryness. As their eyes met, Meg felt certain he could sense her attraction to him and realized that far more than personality differences concerned her. "If we're not perfectly comfortable with each other, as well as with the format we choose, putting in a full shift in that booth could become a real strain. Even in the short time we shared today, I managed to aggravate you over and over again."

"Well, for Pete's sake! You were talking about my days in diapers. That's damned undignified, Meg!"

"But listeners loved it. Don't you see what I mean about us working together? If nothing else, your blood pressure is going to go up."

"After the routine you pulled at KSUN, you need someone to keep your high spirits in check."

"Meaning you?" She sighed. He was so damned pragmatic! They truly were opposites. Yet the physical attraction was still there.

Hormones! All they ever did was cause trouble. They should be either something one acquired along with a marriage license, or an extra, purchased at one's option, like snow tires or rear-window defoggers.

"That's right," Kyle said. "I'm more down to earth, so I would temper your style a bit." He came around to the front of the desk, standing inches away from her. "Quite by accident we've stumbled on to something that could help me keep this station on the air." He paused. "Like it or not, the listeners *did* enjoy us. I would never have chosen to place myself in the limelight this way, but I can handle it, as long as I know I'm also doing something worthwhile for the community. If we make sure our show really serves a purpose, in addition to being entertaining, then I'll be completely satisfied."

Serves a purpose? That sounded ominous. What did he want to do, turn it into an educational broadcast with some country western music on the side? If so, this job definitely wasn't for her. She was a deejay, not a teacher.

But before she could protest, Kyle continued. "There's something you have to understand about me and the reason I started this station. For years I worked for one of the major oil companies in Houston. I started off as a field engineer and climbed all the way up to vice president in charge of foreign operations. I earned a very lucrative salary, but I found that money alone wasn't enough to keep me happy. I wanted to accomplish more than showing a profit on the yearly balance sheets."

He returned to his desk chair. "I grew up in this town. I decided to come back because I felt I could make a difference here."

His vibrant expression communicated an enthusiasm and conviction that was contagious. Call it charismatic, or magnetic, but there was something about this man that sent shivers up Meg's spine. Trying to distract herself, she focused on the forearms exposed by his partially rolled-up shirtsleeves. But his bronzed skin dusted with golden brown hair further fanned the dormant fires within her.

With effort she forced herself to concentrate on what he was saying.

"I can reach all sorts of people through KHAY," he continued, with excitement. "I have an opportunity to help make this town better, to make a positive contribution to a place I care a great deal about. When I bought this station eight months ago, I fulfilled a fantasy. Ever since I put myself through college by working for radio stations, I've wanted to own one. This is my chance to do it all."

"But what's wrong with just entertaining people?" Meg asked softly. "Give them good music and a good show, and you've added some sunshine to their lives."

"Not completely. I want this station to take an active part in getting people involved in community affairs. I still remember hearing about a certain station in Utah that sponsored a barn raising when a farmer's barn burned down. Everyone in the town showed up to help. I want KHAY to promote that kind of closeness, to become an integral part of this town. If it's strictly an entertainment station, we'll be just like KLUV, and that's not what I have in mind at all."

"KLUV?"

He scowled. "The station Monica Hanrahan owns and runs. She's like one of the great whites they spoke of in that movie about sharks," he added acerbically.

Meg laughed. "Your competition, huh?"

"The woman is not to be believed. She owns everything from cattle ranches to oil wells. Some of it she inherited from her husband, Carl, after he died, but she's turned his assets into an empire."

"She sounds like one heck of a lady," Meg replied, a bit in awe.

"Oh, there's no denying her accomplishments, but I can't stand a woman who goes around acting like she's queen of the world. She stops at nothing to get what she wants." His expression took on a thoughtful aspect. "I can still remember when she decided she wanted *me!*"

Meg chuckled. It was obvious he had revealed far more than he had intended. His discomfiture was evident in the way he shifted uneasily in his chair. She recognized the symptoms, having often been in the same position herself. "I would have thought you'd be flattered," she said.

"You haven't met her. Wait."

The intercom buzzed, interrupting him. "Monica Hanrahan is out here to see you. She heard your—"

Spring Madness 21

Before the receptionist could finish, a tall stately blonde breezed into the office. She was wearing designer denims and a matching blue shirt that had undoubtedly been purchased at an expensive boutique. She was quite pretty, but there was a hard edge to her features that lessened her attractiveness. "I hate to wait for introductions, Kyle." Her eyes darted over Meg with a mixture of curiosity and amusement. "You wouldn't be Meg Randall, would you?"

"I am." Whatever Monica Hanrahan might be, she was not shy and retiring. In some ways Meg was intrigued by her. She instinctively liked any woman who could take charge of a situation simply by walking into a room. It was an ability she hoped to acquire herself someday.

"You're very good on the air, and attractive, too." Monica smiled. "Of course, I *have* heard about you." Her tone let Meg know she was aware of the events that had cost her her job in Phoenix. "You might turn out to be just what Kyle needs. It would be fun if KHAY started giving KLUV some serious competition."

"It seems to me that's the last thing you'd want," Meg replied guardedly.

Monica gave an idle toss of her hand. "I love challenges. Being number one is a lot more fun if you get to engage a worthy adversary and defeat him in the process."

Meg found herself smiling. "What makes you so sure you'd win?"

"Because the alternative, losing, is not acceptable to me. I never settle for it; consequently, I always win."

"Persistence, then, is your key to success," Meg said, thoroughly enjoying Monica's unabashed self-assurance." Kyle, meanwhile, was sitting back in his chair, eyeing both women warily.

"And what if you met an opponent who shared your philosophy?" Meg continued. "One who was just as persistent?"

"Then it would be a magnificent fight." Monica's head whipped around, and she leveled a challenging stare at

Kyle. "But the outcome would be the same—I'd win."

"Monica doesn't suffer from an overabundance of humility, Meg, as I'm sure you've noticed by now." The icy tone in Kyle's voice surprised Meg.

Monica laughed. "Kyle and I have one major philosophical difference," she explained. "When I see something I want, I take it. Kyle, on the other hand, weighs all the factors, then proceeds with such caution that by the time he figures out what he wants, the opportunity is gone."

"That's not quite true, Monica," Kyle drawled with deceptive unconcern. Meg sensed the steellike anger beneath his calm demeanor. "I just don't have the resources you have to gamble with—or the unscrupulousness. Besides, I've worked for everything I've achieved."

Only the tightness in Monica's smile betrayed the fact that Kyle's statement had angered her. "You don't call being married to a man like Carl for twelve years payment enough?"

"Everyone knows Carl wasn't easy to deal with, but—"

"I spent most of my adult life living with a man who insisted on making every decision for me," she interrupted. "I loved him, so I let him manage my life completely. It was better than the arguments that ensued every time I tried to assert myself. But I paid a high price for keeping the peace between us. When he died, I didn't even know how to balance a checkbook." Her eyes narrowed. "But I made it. In fact, I've practically doubled the worth of the estate he left me. I'm not a shrinking violet anymore, and I don't have to apologize for myself. If I want something, you'd better believe I'll reach out and take it. I deserve everything I can get."

"No matter what the cost to others?" Kyle asked flatly.

"Don't be overly dramatic, dear," she shot back. "I don't cheat people. I'm just a darned good businesswoman."

"You call a deal like the one you struck with Marc Cooper, the former owner of KLUV, ethical? You didn't pay him a tenth of what the station was worth."

She shrugged. "I made him an offer, and he accepted it. I didn't twist his arm."

"You knew his financial situation."

"Precisely. That's what made it a wise business investment for me. If a friend of yours had done the same thing, you'd have praised him on his business acumen."

Kyle scowled.

"And remember, after I started to manage it, KLUV became the number one station in this part of the state." She glanced at Meg. "You two make quite a team on the air, but even with that stroke of luck, you won't beat me in the ratings. And that means KHAY won't be able to command the advertising prices needed to keep it running." She turned her attention back to Kyle. "You'd do yourself a favor if you'd merge with me. I'm offering you a fair price. And you'd still be able to manage KHAY—as long as you followed my guidelines, of course." She sat down on a corner of Kyle's desk and gave him a long look. "If you wait until you *have* to sell, my price won't be as generous."

Kyle remained unmoved by her threat. With calm self-confidence he replied, "If you really thought I was going to fail, you wouldn't make me an offer. You'd wait until you could buy KHAY dirt-cheap. What worries you is that I'll push you right out of the number one position, and you'll end up facing quite a drop in revenue. I know KLUV is your pet project," he continued. "After spending all the money you did bringing in those big-name deejays, you can't stand the thought of being second best."

"Let's just say I'm not staying up nights worrying about it," she replied with a chuckle.

Meg bit her lip to keep from laughing. Kyle could be a bit high-handed, such as when he had insisted that they become a team, but seeing him confront someone who wielded as much power as Monica did was proving to be quite entertaining.

Apparently noticing Meg's reaction, Kyle scowled and

said sharply, "Monica, is there something specific you wanted? Because, in case you haven't noticed, you've interrupted a business meeting."

She smiled. "I see I've struck a nerve. How delightful. You look very cute when you're angry."

Hearing such a traditionally chauvinistic line coming from Monica made Meg laugh.

Monica winked at her. "They can dish it out, but they can't take it, can they?"

Without another word she sauntered out of Kyle's office.

Kyle rose slowly, closed the door, and returned to his desk. Meg avoided his eyes, afraid that if she looked at him she'd laugh again.

"You think this is amusing, don't you?" he accused.

"I think Monica is absolutely formidable," Meg replied candidly. "In fact, she's exactly the kind of person I hope to become someday."

"That's the most disgusting thing I've ever heard anyone wish upon herself." Kyle's eyes flashed with anger, and he muttered an oath. Then, with slow deliberation, he schooled his expression into one of calm neutrality.

His strong reaction surprised her. She sensed it had taken all of his willpower to calm his temper. "I realize she's not the type of woman men usually like," she ventured, unwilling to alter her opinion to please him, "but you've got to admire her. She's got nerve. I'd never have strolled into someone's office the way she did."

"That's because you're not rude, whereas she doesn't know the meaning of the word."

Meg started to reply, then lapsed into silence. It wasn't smart to antagonize her boss on the first day. "All right. Let's get back to what we were discussing—my job here at the station."

"Do you accept the idea of us working together as a team?" he asked.

As she looked directly at him, her pulse began to hammer. What would it be like to be held in his embrace? The attraction that crackled between them was like a wild

Spring Madness 25

wind buffeting her. She tried to shatter the spell by breaking contact with his eyes, which held hers captive.

"Are you giving me a choice?" she asked.

"No."

"You're sure?" She felt torn between the desire that flooded her veins and her determination not to give in to his sensuality. Had the room grown considerably warmer? The atmosphere had suddenly become stifling. She fought a sense of alarm as she realized that circumstances had woven an inescapable web around her.

"I'm positive," he insisted.

Still, she hoped against hope that she could intimidate him into backing down. But the silence between them grew heavy. Meg sighed. It wasn't going to work. "In that case, boss, I accept."

"I thought you might," he replied with a satisfied smile.

"Don't gloat, boss. It doesn't become you."

"Don't call me *boss,* and I'm not gloating," he replied, chuckling.

"How soon do you want me to start working?"

"How about tomorrow?" he countered immediately. "I'll switch T.J. to the afternoon time slot, and you and I will share morning drive time."

"All right. Everything I brought from Phoenix is in the trunk of my car, so it shouldn't be hard to get settled—once I find a place to live." She cocked her head. "This is your town. Any suggestions?"

"As a matter of fact, I know of an elderly lady who's looking for someone to share her home with. She lives in a beautiful old house about five miles from here. She wouldn't charge you much."

"Speaking of expenses, what about my salary?"

He scribbled a number on a piece of paper and handed it to her.

"You're kidding! This is barely poverty level! Surely you can do better that this."

"That's the point. I can't." He rubbed his chin. "I realize you couldn't live on this sum in Phoenix, but it's adequate for this area, believe me."

She stared at the figure and sighed. Once this job got her back into the broadcasting scene, she could always move on to better things later. It wasn't as if she had received dozens of other offers. There was no denying it; she was stuck. "All right," she said.

"See? We *can* get along." Kyle stood, extended his hand, and clasped hers in a firm handshake. His eyes probed hers with sensual warmth. "Welcome to KHAY."

The heat of his palm seeped into her, searing her skin and igniting her senses with a slow fire.

Feeling uneasy, she reminded herself of the danger of being attracted to him. Already he reminded her of her ex-husband, Mike. Surely she wasn't foolish enough to allow another manipulative man into her life. Kyle knew how to combine power with charm to get what he wanted from people. Whether he was attractive or not, she would have to find a way to maintain a professional distance from him.

"Thank you, Kyle," she said in a cool voice. The first step would be never to lower her defenses around him. Perhaps she would be forced to make compromises in her style of broadcasting and in the nature of her job, but she would never go any further than that. Her private life would remain her own, and no one, especially not Kyle Rager, would intrude upon it.

But his next words almost robbed her of her resolve as soon as she had made it.

"You're extraordinary beautiful and talented," he said in a sensually charged whisper that stopped her heart. "This is bound to be an exciting partnership, Meg Randall."

Desire flared between them. She stifled a groan. Why did this have to happen to her? Why couldn't Kyle Rager have been a married man in his sixties, balding, with a girth that equaled the dimensions of a football field?

He stepped so close that she could feel the heat radiating from his body. The thumping of her heart seemed deafening in the sudden silence.

"Don't close your mind to all the possibilities too soon, Meg," he pleaded. "We're about to become allies, not adversaries." He brushed a strand of hair away from her face.

The fleeting touch made her flesh tingle, but she cleared her throat and said emphatically, "On the air, we'll be allies. That's what partners should be." Her voice cracked slightly. "But whether we *both* choose to be friends... that, Mr. Rager, remains to be seen."

Chapter 3

MEG DROVE HER beat-up Chevy down the almost deserted road through the outskirts of Cabezon. The desert mesas were empty except for a few scattered houses. Following the directions that Patsy, KHAY's receptionist, had given her, she continued down the road even after the pavement gave way to gravel.

Meg frowned, trying to figure out what the young secretary's puzzled, then knowing, smile could have meant when Meg had shown her the address she'd wanted to locate. Had Kyle sent her to someone disreputable? It didn't seem likely.

As she reached the top of the next hill, she glanced down at the endless panorama below. A wooden frame house in an incongruous Victorian style of architecture stood out against a background of sagebrush and cactus. Knowing she was alone on the road, Meg pulled over to the right side and stopped.

The scene was beautiful in its starkness. The distant

purple mountains seemed much closer in the clear desert air, but the scene also made her feel lonely. No wonder the elderly woman who lived there wanted to take in boarders.

Meg weighed her options. Was she ready to live in such an isolated place?

She certainly wouldn't lose anything by taking a look. Easing her car back onto the road, she drove the rest of her way to the house and parked in the dirt driveway.

When she got out of the car, an overweight, well-groomed, white-haired woman in her middle sixties came out to greet her. "I'm Kate Brown. You must be Meg Randall," she said enthusiastically, shaking Meg's hand with surprising firmness. "Kyle called me a while ago and said you might be stopping by. You're even prettier than he said you were. And tall, just like him. When he told me you were new to our area, I began to get worried. I wasn't sure you'd find me even if you did decide to come see the house."

"I got directions from Kyle's secretary," Meg said, giving the woman a reassuring smile. "But I've got to be honest. When I saw how isolated you are out here, I almost turned back."

The woman nodded. "Most young people won't live here for that reason. Heaven knows Cabezon is small enough, but at least by living in town they're close to their other friends, and it's easier for them to socialize." She smiled ruefully. "Once you get out this far, there's nothing except desert for miles around."

Meg followed her to the front door. The stately, two-story home looked comfortably spacious. "It seems strange to find a house with this type of architecture out here," she said, thinking out loud.

"My husband built it for me years ago, soon after we came to New Mexico. I hated to leave my home in South Carolina, but he had been offered a job with the Bureau of Land Management, and this is the area they wanted us to relocate to. For months I tried to convince him to quit and go back home with me. Then I began to accept

Spring Madness

the fact that he'd never do that. We had come to the Southwest for good. In return he built this house for us. It's a replica of the one I grew up in near Charleston."

"You've lived here for a long time, then," Meg ventured.

"Practically all my adult life," Kate replied. "Of course the past eight years, ever since Jim died, have been the hardest. I wasn't used to being alone. Still, after awhile I got used to it. It wasn't until recently that I realized I didn't have to be lonely if I didn't want to. That's when I decided to open up the house to boarders. It was my nephew's idea, really. He thinks I shouldn't live alone this far out of town at my age."

"I bet he cares a great deal about you," Meg observed. Something about the way Kate Brown had confided in her touched Meg's heart, and she found herself liking the woman who'd been a stranger only seconds ago. "Do you have other boarders with you now?" Meg asked.

Kate gestured for her to go inside. "My nephew visits from time to time, but that's all. He's got his own home on the other side of Cabezon."

From the foyer Meg glanced at the enormous living room. She smelled the lemony scent of furniture polish and caught the gleam of waxed wooden floors.

"As you can see, it's too big a house for one person," Kate pointed out.

"It's spotless," Meg commented, wondering how anyone who lived in a desert filled with drifting sand and dust managed to keep it from filtering inside.

"I'm a good housekeeper, and I'm also a good cook," Kate said. "Your meals will all be home-cooked. Your rent includes breakfast and dinner."

Staying there was starting to sound expensive. "I guess I better ask how much you charge. It's a lovely home, and having home-cooked meals sounds wonderful, but I'm going to be living on a very strict budget."

"Let me show you your room first."

Meg followed Kate to the upstairs hallway. She opened a door. "This is it."

A large ornate canopied bed stood in the center. To one side was a small nightstand on which had been placed a glass vase containing a single red rose. On the other side a small round table was covered by a crocheted mantle. The handmade quilt on the bed had been crafted in ivory and shades of light blue to match the walls.

"Now I *know* I can't afford to stay here," Meg said weakly.

"I don't charge much, really," Kate replied. "It's two hundred dollars a month for room and board."

Meg could scarcely believe her ears. There had to be a catch. "Are there rules or any chores that I'll be expected to do?"

"I'll keep your room clean, but you'll be responsible for your own laundry."

"That sounds fair. Anything else?"

"I won't allow men upstairs. If you want to entertain boyfriends or male guests, you'll have to use the parlor downstairs."

Meg almost laughed with relief as she tried to picture herself in the genteel setting. "It's perfect!"

"So you'll stay?"

"I'd be delighted."

"In that case, why don't you come downstairs with me? I just baked some apple turnovers. After you sign the rental agreement, we'll celebrate by snacking and sharing a cup of coffee. What do you say?"

"I'd love to."

Meg followed Kate downstairs. Sitting at a round table in the cozy kitchen, she signed a three-month lease. "I guess we're all set, then," she said. "After we finish eating, I'll go get the trunks out of my car. They're enormous, and just about everything I own is packed in them."

"Take your time. My nephew should be along shortly, and he'll be glad to give you a hand taking your luggage upstairs. By the way, in case you ever get locked out and can't get hold of me, he has a spare key in his desk at the office. Since you both work at the same place, it should be easy to borrow his." She poured them both a cup of coffee and made herself comfortable in the chair opposite Meg's. "I meant to tell you earlier. You two sure make a great radio team."

It took Meg several seconds to understand. "Wait a minute. Your nephew can't be—"

At that instant the back door flew open. "Hello, Aunt Kate!" Kyle exclaimed, reaching for a turnover.

Meg sat alone in her room trying to sort out her thoughts. The idea of living with Kyle's aunt bothered her. Now, she'd never be able to get her new boss out of her mind! And what if she had a disagreement with Kate? Would that affect her status at work? It simply hadn't been fair of Kyle to neglect telling her that the woman who was renting out a room was his own aunt.

A knock sounded on her door. "Who is it?" she asked, suspecting the answer.

"It's Kyle. I want to talk to you."

"Go away. I'm not dressed." She stared at her floor-length lounge robe. Though bare-shouldered, it was modest enough to greet anyone in. Nonetheless, she wasn't going to confront Kyle until she had a very definite plan of action in mind.

"You don't have to get dressed because of me. I like undressed women," came his instant reply.

She rolled her eyes. Taking a deep breath, she opened the door just enough to peer out. "Is something wrong?"

"Not at all." His eyes dropped to the base of her throat, then focused on her bare shoulders. Her stomach fluttered. One hand rose to her throat as she tried to force herself to remain calm under his scrutinizing gaze. "Why don't you let me help you move your trunks upstairs?" he suggested softly.

"I have a small suitcase with me. The trunks can wait until later."

"Okay. Then we'll go out. I'll buy you a nice dinner, show you the area..."

"In the dark?" She gave him an exasperated look.

"All right, no sightseeing. We'll just have a nice, leisurely dinner, talk, and get to know each other."

"That's a bad way to start off our *business* relationship."

"Good," he replied, ignoring her comment. "I'll be by in an hour to pick you up."

Before Meg had a chance to protest, Kyle strode down the hall. Meg sighed. She had already signed a rental agreement, so she couldn't move out now. What to do, then? The situation was bound to lead to all sorts of complications. It even made her feel awkward around Kate. There was only one answer. During dinner with Kyle she'd explain how she felt and ask that he speak to his aunt about letting her out of the lease.

After showering and changing into a pair of black slacks and a soft yellow mohair sweater, Meg brushed her hair until it fell softly around her shoulders, then decided she'd look more commanding if she tied it back, away from her face.

Taking one final look in the mirror, she decided to meet Kyle downstairs. The thought of his coming up to her bedroom made her uncomfortable.

She opened her door—and stepped right up against Kyle's massive chest. "What the..." In an instant she was vividly aware of each hard plane and contour of his powerful torso. His warmth enveloped her in a comforting cocoon as a variety of sensations flooded her mind, momentarily obscuring the impulse to step away.

"Oops." He laughed as he grasped her shoulders and steadied her. "I just came up to see if you were ready. I guess you are."

For several heartbeats they stood only inches apart. Meg's desire to step into his embrace was almost overwhelming. Instead, overreacting to the danger signs, she almost jumped away.

"You don't have to be afraid of me, Meg," Kyle said in a voice tinged with regret. "I'm completely harmless around attractive women."

"Said the spider to the fly," she muttered.

"Let's talk this out over dinner." His blue-green eyes focused on her with thrilling intensity.

"I'm not really hungry."

"I am," he cajoled. "You wouldn't want me to try and convince you that I'm not an ogre while my stomach's growling incessantly, would you?"

Despite herself, she laughed. "All right. But let's keep dinner simple."

"There's a café just outside of town that has the best Mexican food in the world. It's not fancy, but no one ever leaves hungry."

"Perfect."

The drive from Kate's house to the restaurant took less than twenty minutes. The building resembled an old-fashioned Mexican hacienda. They were escorted to a large patio filled with tables adorned with colorful umbrellas. In the center a small stone fountain added a musical cascade of water.

After ordering a carafe of wine and two enchilada dinners, Kyle settled back. "Okay. I guess we'd better get things out into the open," he said with resignation. "Are you angry because I didn't tell you I was sending you to my aunt's house?"

"Are you aware that you've put me in a very difficult position?" Meg countered.

"You've got a great room and a very nice woman to share a large, beautiful home with. I don't think I've cheated you."

"Kyle, you're my boss, and she's your aunt!"

"I'm aware of that," he said, studying her with amusement. "In fact, we both are. So what?"

"I'll feel as if I'm on the job twenty-four hours a day. What if Kate and I have an argument, for instance? How will that affect my relationship with you at work?"

"Is that what's worrying you?" He looked relieved. "I promise that whatever happens between you and Aunt Kate will stay between you two. To be honest, I very much doubt she'd ever say anything to me about you. So unless you brought me into it, I'd never know."

Meg shifted uncomfortably under his steady gaze. "I'm not sure about this."

"I'll tell you what. Let's finish dinner. You can think about what we've said, then tell me what you've decided when we return to Aunt Kate's. Fair enough?"

She couldn't argue with that. If only there weren't so many pros and cons to speculate on. "All right."

The strain between them was evident throughout dinner. She scarcely tasted any of the food as she went over her options, trying to decide what to do. Absently she tried to contribute to their conversation, but her thoughts were elsewhere.

"You're miles away, aren't you?" he asked finally.

"I came from Phoenix," she replied absently, finishing the last of her entrée.

He laughed. "That answers my question."

Puzzled, she looked up at him. Had she said something wrong? Her heart stopped. The sympathy mirrored in his face took her completely by surprise.

He repeated what she'd said to him.

She shifted uneasily. "I *am* distracted," she admitted. "But I'm trying to figure out what I should do about living with your aunt. You should understand. You're the one who put me in this predicament."

"I guess I'd better tell you the entire story," he said. "You deserve that much." He seemed to struggle with himself. It was as if he hadn't wanted to broach the subject, yet acknowledged the necessity of doing so. "I'm very fond of Aunt Kate. About two months ago I began to notice that she was getting absentminded. She'd miss appointments and forget people's names—that sort of thing. The doctor said it was simply a result of aging and that there was nothing to be done about it, but I was still concerned about her living all alone so far from town. So, I decided to give up my apartment and convinced her to let me move in as a boarder. Since she was having a bit of difficulty meeting the property taxes and paying the utility bills, she agreed.

"Things worked out well for both of us until construction was finally completed on my own house. It was time for me to go, but I hated the thought of leaving Aunt Kate by herself. I asked her to move in with me, but she wouldn't hear of it. That's when I began looking for someone I felt was trustworthy enough to watch over her and help her out a bit." In silence he watched the waiter fill his coffee cup.

"My intent was not to trick you, Meg. Honest. I knew you'd get a good deal from my Aunt Kate. At the same time, I'd feel better having you live with her."

What could Meg say? She hated to admit it, but his explanation made sense. Had Kate been her aunt, she might have done the same thing.

"You're making me feel like a knight in not-so-shining armor," he said.

"Unfortunately it's not that simple, Kyle. I understand why you acted the way you did, but I hate underhandedness."

His shoulders slumped. "If that's the way you feel, then I'll speak to my aunt as soon as we get back to her house."

"Please don't put words in my mouth," she objected. "I haven't made my decision yet."

He picked up the check. "I'm not going to say another word. That's the closest you've come to an actual *yes*, and for now I'm going to accept that as good fortune."

"Wise move." She moved regally toward the door. At least this time she wasn't going to be easily manipulated.

By the time they returned to Kate's house, Meg had made up her mind. She'd stay. After all, by taking a stand she had proven that the decision had been strictly her choice, not one imposed on her.

"I've decided to stay," she told Kyle as they approached the front door.

"Out on the porch?" He shrugged. "Okay. It's a beautiful evening for it."

She blinked. "No. What I meant is that I've decided to live here."

"That's great!" He started to come closer, but stopped when she took a step back.

"Kyle, there's something you have to understand about me. I don't like being told what to do by anyone."

He sat down on the cushioned swing suspended from the porch rafters. "I've noticed. At the risk of making you angry again, I have to say you're rather touchy on that subject, aren't you?"

"Maybe I am," she conceded.

She had been physically attracted to her ex-husband, Mike Randall, in much the same way that she was attracted to Kyle. But all those feelings had ever done was trap her in a marriage that should never have taken place. A physical attraction, she had learned, was far from love, and not enough to bind two people together. Was she on the road to repeating the same mistake?

Mike had been a skillful manipulator. He had managed to coerce her into doing almost anything he wanted. He had taught her how a man could use sex as a weapon of control.

She faced Kyle once again. She'd never be that docile and easily manipulated again. "Kyle, I have very good reasons for being the way I am. Maybe someday I'll tell you a bit about myself and you'll understand."

"Come over here and sit on the swing with me," he said quietly. "We can talk now. I'd like to get to know you much better, Meg."

"I can't confide in someone I'm not completely comfortable with."

"Then why not just relax and enjoy the evening with me? It's a beautiful night."

She walked to the railing of the veranda. "It is."

"I love sitting out here," he said. "Somehow it feels as if I've stepped back in time."

"I've always wondered what it would have been like to have grown up around the turn of the century. I'd love to wear pretty long gowns and have a dashing beau come courting me." She looked away from him, suddenly embarassed.

Spring Madness

"You're a romantic at heart, I see."

"In some ways."

"Will you come sit beside me, and just relax?" he pleaded.

Meg laughed and acquiesced. She seated herself a discreet distance from him and began to propel the swing back and forth with her feet. "I've never lived any place where it was this quiet."

"Do you like it?"

"Yes," she replied at length. "I really do. It's soothing."

A mantle of darkness enfolded the mesa. Moonlight cast eerie patterns of shadows on the ground, dappling the tumbleweed and softening their craggy edges with a gentle glow.

"Are you cold?" Kyle asked when a breeze gently began to rustle the wild grass.

"The desert is always cool at night, but my sweater feels just right."

He edged a little closer to her. "Well, it wouldn't hurt to snuggle up a little for warmth. I'm a bit chilly."

Meg avoided his eyes but a smile tugged at the corners of her mouth. "I wouldn't want you to catch cold." Sitting there with Kyle, she suddenly felt like a teenager in an old movie. Anytime now an adult's voice would call out to her, telling her to come inside because it was past her bedtime.

"I'm glad you're no longer looking at me as if I were the enemy, Meg," Kyle said quietly. "I'm not, you know. I really do like you."

She felt the warmth of his breath against the nape of her neck. He moved his arm from the back of the swing and draped it over her shoulders in a protectively affectionate way. She noticed he had moved closer, leaving the barest gap between them. "I wish you could see yourself through my eyes," he said. "Maybe then you'd understand how enticing you really are."

Wispy tendrils of desire coursed through her. She wanted to sample the kiss she knew would be hers if she only met his eyes. But it was much too dangerous to give in to such pulsing excitement. He was beguiling her senses and playing havoc with her reason. Worst of all, she didn't really want to fight the feelings. The woman in her longed to yield to the seductive temptation he offered.

He seemed to guess her thoughts. "It's spring," he murmured. "A special time of year." He tilted her chin upward until he had captured her eyes. "I wish moments like these could be stored away like fragile petals between pages of a book. You're so beautiful."

Moving his lips slowly over hers, he coaxed her to yield to the intoxicating magic flowering between them. With slow, patient tenderness, he savored her sweetness.

Meg's pulse raced wildly as she submitted to his kiss. She wrapped her arms around his neck and brought him against her. Her fingers curled into his thick golden hair as her tongue entwined with his in a delicious primitive dance.

He stroked her neck with erotic skill. A slow, consuming fire began to spread through her, a desire so strong that it frightened her and gave her the courage to push away from him. She stood up and walked to the steps leading down from the porch.

"I'm sorry, Kyle," she murmured, turning to face him. "I shouldn't have let that happen."

"There's nothing to be sorry about." His voice was deep, his manner infinitely patient.

Tearing her gaze from his glittering eyes, she searched for some way to break the aura of enchantment that charged the air between them.

Yearning still tingled within her, declaring war against her determination not to return to his side. She stared at his hands, wondering what it would be like to feel them intimately caressing her. If the masculine aggression she had previously sensed in him was any indication, he'd be a demanding lover. Instinct told her he'd also be intoxicatingly gentle. It would be so easy to lose herself in his embrace.

"I like the way you're looking at me," he said huskily.

She choked. "I don't know what you're talking about."

"I think you do," he replied calmly. He strode toward her on the front porch steps.

Meg's pulse fluttered like a leaf caught in an autumn breeze. The closer he came, the less clear her thoughts grew. She was losing her mind; that's all there was to it. "What are you doing?" she blurted out.

He paused. "I was going to suggest we go to your car and get your trunks," he drawled, clearly amused. "If you're going to live here, you'll want the rest of your things."

Feeling foolish, she tried to cover up her embarrassment. "That's a great idea. I'm all for making you suffer."

"Suffer?" Kyle walked beside her to the car. As he waited for her to find her keys, he gave her a suspicious look. "That doesn't bode well at all," he mused.

A few minutes later they were struggling with the first of the large overseas trunks, carrying it up the porch steps and across the foyer.

"Now I know what you meant about suffering," Kyle muttered, setting down his end. "When I volunteered to help, I didn't realize you'd filled each one with concrete."

Meg looked up the steep stairs and grimaced. "The worst is yet to come. Taking this trunk up to my room is going to be a killer."

"I'll tell you what," he ventured. "I'll push it up. All you have to do is hold on to the handle from the top and steer. Okay?"

"Are you sure we both shouldn't push?"

"Trust me. By the way, if I survive this ordeal, rest assured that you've more than paid me back for any transgressions I might have committed." He rubbed his back with one hand. "Seriously, Meg, what in the world do you have in there?"

"Just clothes and things," she replied with a shrug. "The usual."

Through narrowed eyes, he regarded her with exaggerated suspicion. "Dead bodies, that's what it is. You're smuggling dead bodies in there," he teased. "Is there something important you left out of your résumé?"

She laughed. "Men are supposed to like lifting heavy things for women. It lets them show off."

"To carry this, you need a platoon of marines." He sat down on the bottom step with a heavy thump.

"Good heavens, Kyle, it isn't that heavy." Tugging on the strap on one side, she pulled the trunk up a couple of steps. But her muscles screamed under the strain. Her fingers grew numb as she concentrated on maintaining her grasp. When she jerked the trunk up the next step, her arm exploded in pain. She stood very still, hoping the sensation would pass, but instead, with dismay she realized she was losing her grip. The handle slid from her fingers. "Oh, no!" she cried.

Kyle leaped to his feet. "Wait."

It happened in an instant. She watched helplessly as the trunk thundered downward and crashed into Kyle, knocking him backward onto the floor.

"Kyle!" Meg ran down the stairs and crouched by his side. Afraid to move him or the trunk that rested against him, she grazed his cheek in a feather-light caress. "What should I do? Are you all right?"

He groaned, then with one powerful motion pushed the trunk off himself, taking in several deep breaths.

There were no visible signs of an injury, Meg noted gratefully as she studied the flat, hard muscles exposed by his torn shirt. An intoxicating breathlessness seized her as she became conscious of his rippling muscles as he cautiously tested his limbs.

"If I told you I was near death," he said, placing one hand on her waist, "would you honor my final wish and give me another kiss?"

She trembled at the warmth of his palm on her skin. His invitation teased her imagination, rekindling the embers of her desire. But she had no intention of giving in to it. "I won't comply with your request because you're not close to dying," she said. "However, if I dropped the trunk on you again..."

He scrambled to his feet. "You're a tough woman, Meg," he said with a laugh. Apparently uninjured, he grabbed hold of the strap and began to haul the trunk up the rest of the stairs.

Chapter 4

MEG PLACED THE next tape in the machine. As music began to flow over the airwaves, she turned off her microphone and sat back. "We're doing just fine. Don't worry."

"I *knew* we should have been more prepared," Kyle replied. "This constant need to ad-lib is putting extra pressure on us. Maybe we should work from a script next time."

"A script?" she repeated, horrified. "You've got to be kidding!" She closed her eyes, struggling to keep her temper in check. "The problem is you're so uptight about broadcasting live, you aren't allowing yourself to develop an on-the-air personality. Just relax a bit, and you'll see that there isn't anything to worry about."

"Meg, your impulsiveness is going to give me white hair."

As the machine's red light came on, indicating that the song was almost over, Meg switched on the microphone and, with an impish grin, said, "We seem to have a problem in the booth, ladies and gentlemen. Kyle's worried that you might not like the way our program's going. How about calling in and giving him some tips on how to relax? At the same time you can tell us how you like the show so far."

Kyle glowered darkly at her. As soon as she placed the next tape on the machine and the music began anew, he exclaimed, "You're doing it to me again, aren't you?"

She laughed. "Weren't you the one who told me never to change a winning game? Well, it worked last time, didn't it?"

He gave her a long, wary look. "Be honest, Meg. Are you trying to give me a coronary right here in this booth so you can work solo, like you wanted all along?" As she started to reach for the mike, he growled, "And if you ask the audience for their opinion on this, I'm going to wring your neck."

She smiled sweetly. The instant the song was over, she told their listeners, "Ladies and gentlemen, Kyle is threatening to wring my neck if I don't stop bothering you folks by asking for your opinion all the time. How do you feel about that?"

Her eyes twinkled with mischief as she started the next set of musical selections. "How's that, boss?"

He was about to answer when the telephone lights began to glow. Once again calls came in one right after the other. The first person Meg put on the line suggested they play more rock music and claimed Meg had a sexy voice. Kyle laughed as Meg politely thanked him and switched to another caller.

"Kyle," a woman said over the telephone, "you should be thankful you've got a partner like Meg. She keeps it lively for us. No offense, but you *do* have a tendency to be rather stodgy."

"Me?" he asked with mock indignation. "You've got it all wrong. I'm the stone railing that keeps this young lady from going over the edge."

Surprised, Meg laughed. "Again there you have it. The awful truth comes out. Kyle Rager is a chauvinist."

Spring Madness

His eyes met hers with an intense warmth that set her heart racing.

"I don't think so. I'm just protective of women," he drawled. "Don't you like that, Meg? I would have thought that, even though the age of chivalry is dead, women would still appreciate a man who's willing to stand up for them in times of trouble."

His words melted through her like liquid gold, making her skin suffuse with warmth. The words lodged in her throat, but she finally managed to answer him. "Yes, but the problem comes in when a man stands *in the way* and becomes a roadblock instead."

"Someone with your temperament would never have that problem. Take it from me, ladies and gentlemen," he quipped into the mike. "It would be easier to hold back a bulldozer with a rubber band than it would be to stop Meg once she's made up her mind about something."

"I'm confused," Meg told their audience good-naturedly. "Is he actually saying that I intimidate him?"

Kyle laughed. "Heck, you don't have to ask them that. I confess. You scare the devil out of me."

Meg put the next musical selection into the machine. "On that note, we'll switch back to some music. Stay tuned for the next installment of the Rager and Randall feud."

The moment she switched off her microphone, Meg's eyes locked with Kyle's. "Why is it that I find the idea of intimidating you so appealing?" she teased.

"Because deep down you're terrified of me, and turnabout's fair play?" he suggested with a sardonic grin, his eyes assessing her warmly.

His arrogant smile infuriated her. "Nice try, but it would take lots more than you to worry me."

He moved his chair closer to her in a deliberate attempt to rattle her composure. "How about you and me, together?"

"Now, there's a thought guaranteed to give me nightmares for months," Meg joked, determined not to let him see how his offhanded comment had affected her. She had to build up better defenses against his easy charm and the masculine sensuality that ravaged her emotions. Forcing herself to concentrate on her job, she switched the microphone over to the adjoining booth, where their newscaster stood waiting for his cue. Then she leaned back in her chair and sighed. "Kyle, why do you insist on baiting me all the time?"

"Isn't that what you're doing to me?" He shrugged. "At least I try not to do it while we're on the air."

"How very kind."

"You don't appreciate me." He gave her a look of despair that lacked all sincerity. "Well, in that case, no more Mister Nice Guy."

She glanced at him quickly. Had she inadvertently precipitated some kind of serious competition between them? There was no time to find out. Receiving the cue from the newscaster, she switched the controls back to her console.

Kyle spoke into his microphone before she could say anything. "Meg tells me I'm no fun, ladies and gentlemen. Meanwhile, I want to ask her out on a date with me. How do I get her to say yes?"

She mouthed the words "Are you crazy?" Then she said aloud, "The problem is that a fun date for Kyle means spending the evening playing checkers."

"Folks, this is getting interesting." He gave her a sly smile. "And what's fun for you, Meg?"

Her mind went blank. For an instant all she could see was an image of her and Kyle lying naked on a soft fur rug, passionately making love.

"Well?" he goaded playfully.

She ran her tongue over suddenly dry lips. She needed an answer—one that the people of Cabezon would appreciate. "Horseback riding," she replied hastily.

"At night?" Kyle laughed. "There you have it. Meg Randall's a real country girl at heart. Never mind that she and the horse would have to wear miners' helmets to see where they were going."

She felt her face burn. The audience undoubtedly

thought she was an idiot. "Who says a date has to be at night, Kyle? Unless you're a vampire, it shouldn't matter."

"All right," he conceded. "On a regular, nighttime type of date—is that specific enough for you?—what do you consider fun?"

"Plenty of things," she retorted, hating herself for the inane reply.

"Name one."

He wasn't going to let her off the hook. She pursed her lips thoughtfully. "I know!"

"Hey, and it only took you thirty minutes to think of it," he baited her. "What a way with words. Who's got a problem with being fun on a date, I ask you, ladies and gentlemen?"

She scowled at him. "I've got the perfect date. Rent a really scary movie, pop a barrel full of popcorn, and we watch the movie on your video player."

"Do we get to snuggle?" he added in a provocative voice.

"That depends on the movie. If you rent something like *Attack of the Deadly Cucumbers,* chances are I'll be too busy throwing vegetables at you."

"How about *The Slime Monster That Ate Greenland?*" he suggested.

"I like to be scared, but completely grossed out is something else. For this one, do you need an aspirin, gallons of antacid, and one of those cute little paper bags they give you in airplanes?"

"Hey, you're the one who prefers scary movies. I like westerns myself."

"You just like to see bandits getting their big black sombreros stomped into the ground."

"See that? You *do* understand me."

"And on that note, ladies and gentlemen," she said brightly, "we'll go back to our program."

As the music began to play, Kyle said, "You know, all this ad-libbing is charming, but this isn't the way I want this show to run."

"What's the matter with it?" she asked, turning in her chair to face him. "I thought we were doing just fine."

"I want more than music and cute dialogue, Meg. I want this station to offer something constructive to our listeners."

"You're still thinking about your community projects, right?"

He nodded. "We've got to get the program going in that direction. I think I've got an idea, too. Just follow my lead."

"Are you sure you know what you're doing?"

"Of course I do. Just give me a few minutes to work out the details."

Kyle scribbled some notes furiously as the cart machine played its selections. When the fifteen-minute segment was over, he took the microphone in hand. "Meg and I have been trying to come up with a community project that KHAY can sponsor—something that will benefit all of us. With that in mind, I've got an idea. How about getting everyone together for a Clean Up Cabezon Day? We'll ask neighborhoods to organize patrols to clean up vacant lots and unsightly yards in their areas."

"Cabezon won't be clean until you direct our public-spirited citizens to your car," Meg interjected mischievously. "It's a real eyesore, people. I save on pencils and paper by writing messages to Kyle in the dirt."

"My car is *not* that dirty!" he protested.

"That's what they all say," she teased back. "Be honest. I'll bet you can't tell me whether your car is blue or gray."

"It's a beautiful sky-blue," he answered defensively. "And it's my pride and joy."

"Well, your pride and joy has approximately eighteen inches of dust on it."

"No, it doesn't."

"I'm not the only one who leaves messages on your hood. I read what another inspired person wrote on your back windshield. Would you believe it said, 'Condemned

Spring Madness 51

by Order of the Board of Health'?"

"I saw that, too," Kyle replied dryly. "Admit it, Meg, that was your handiwork."

"Not me, boss."

The next few hours passed quickly. Thoroughly enjoying herself, Meg began to compare how much fun her new job was to how lonely it had been sitting for hours on end by herself in the booth at her old job in Phoenix. Sometimes listener participation had helped pass the time, but for the most part her deejay's work there had been boring. Having Kyle to kid and match wits with was lots more fun. Maybe being part of a team wasn't so bad, after all.

But it was clear that something was disturbing Kyle. By the time they turned the controls over to the arriving disk jockey, his scowl was pronounced.

He exploded as soon as they were out of the booth. "I think my idea for a clean-up day is a good one, but you kept kidding around. Now people will never take it seriously."

"We're supposed to be entertaining the audience, Kyle. That's why you hired me, remember?"

"I wonder if I can plead temporary insanity," he muttered.

"We're doing great! Consider how many people call us during our show. They're so involved, they think of it as *their* show! That's fantastic!"

"I can't work this way, Meg. You're going to have to modify your style."

"Why can't you adapt yours to suit mine?" she asked, following him into his office.

"Because it's my station, and I'm the one who signs your paychecks."

"What happened to not wanting to tamper with success?"

"I'm telling you, I can't operate this way."

He had just seated himself behind the desk when the receptionist entered. "Kyle, there are several people outside milling around your car."

"What?" In an instant he was on his feet, racing to the door.

Meg followed, inches behind him.

As they stepped outside the building, she saw three men and four women all in their early twenties, with buckets and sponges in hand. They were washing Kyle's car!

"What are you people doing?" he asked in surprise.

"We heard how badly you needed a car wash, so we decided to lend our services," explained a thin young man with dark-rimmed glasses. "We thought we'd get your Clean Up Cabezon campaign off to a great start."

Kyle's face brightened. "I don't know what to say." He glanced appreciatively at the small group.

"How about 'thanks'?" one of the girls ventured. "Hey, it's not every day we get to help out celebrities. We'll be glad to call it even if you'll let us take some photographs of you two standing with us after we finish."

"You've got yourself a deal," Kyle replied, taking obvious delight in his newfound celebrity status. "By the way, where are you getting the water?" he asked, puzzled.

"From the gas station across the street," answered a short, dark-haired young woman who looked like a large kewpie doll.

Kyle turned to Meg and, with a look of devilish merriment handed her a bucket of soapy water. "Why don't you go inside and get these nice people some clean, fresh water for my car? That way they won't have to go clear across the street."

Dirty water sloshed out of the bucket. "Is this job listed in my contract?" she muttered sarcastically.

She returned a few minutes later, tripped over one of the parking lot speed bumps, and spilled half of the contents over her tan suede shoes.

One of the young men rushed over to her. "Let me help," he offered.

Aiming her most icy look at Kyle, she accepted gratefully.

Spring Madness 53

Kyle approached her as the group began to work. "You were the one who complained about the dirt on my car," he mischievously reminded her. "I thought it was only fair that you give them a hand."

"Do me a favor, will you?" she retorted. "Don't volunteer me for anything else. Thanks to you I'm going to have to creep around the station in waterlogged shoes."

Just then, a long, booming clap of thunder echoed above them. Kyle glanced up. "Didn't our newscast predict only a twenty percent chance of rain?"

Meg nodded. "It sure did."

Suddenly a strong wind blew, and they were engulfed in an enormous maelstrom of dust and sand.

"Oh, no! The sand's sticking to the car," one of the girls complained. "We should have dried it off more quickly."

A light drizzle began to settle the dust. Soon, however, it turned into a full-fledged rainstorm.

"I don't believe it," said the tallest boy. "Wouldn't it figure? We haven't even finished washing the car and it's starting to rain."

Quickly picking up their cleaning gear, the group sought shelter from the deluge at the rear exit of the station.

"Even if Mother Nature wasn't exactly cooperative," Kyle said, "I really appreciate what you kids tried to do. Since you were all so nice, how about coming inside with us and having some coffee?" Glancing at Meg, he added, "My partner will take care of the arrangements and give you a V.I.P. tour of the radio station."

The group gave a chorus of enthusiastic cheers.

As they entered the building, Meg slipped into step beside Kyle. "What's this about me taking care of all the details? You *are* planning to help, aren't you?"

"I never did get to plug my Clean Up Cabezon Day because you were too busy promoting a car wash," he needled matter-of-factly. "So, as I see it, this party is all yours. Have fun. I'll leave you in her capable hands, then," Kyle told the young people. With a casual wave, he strode down the hall to the exit.

"Wait!" Meg sprang forward. "Where are you going?" she demanded, lowering her voice.

"Home. It's late and I want to get some rest." He waved good-bye to two girls who were peering down the hall from the lounge.

"You're not really leaving, are you?" Meg whispered harshly. "I want to go home, too. If we help each other, the tour will take less time."

"Not for me. I'm leaving now. Enjoy your after-the-car-wash party."

It was futile to argue. Meg watched in exasperation as he opened the door and ran across the rain-soaked parking lot to his car.

"Kyle Rager, I hope your clothes all turn to mold in this rain," she muttered, heading back to the lounge.

It was three in the afternoon by the time Meg returned to Kate's house. Barely awake, she struggled up the stairs. She was halfway to her room when Kate glanced out the kitchen doorway and called, "Would you like me to bring you up a slice of pie? I just made two—cherry, and peach crumb."

Meg closed her eyes and sighed. "Kate, I'm too tired even to eat. I got up at three-thirty so I could be at work at four-thirty. It's been a very long day for me."

"Eat something. You'll feel better."

Too tired to argue, she nodded. "Whatever you say. But then I'm going to take a long nap."

Several minutes later Kate appeared in Meg's doorway with a tray containing a thick slice of peach crumb pie on a plate and a large glass of milk.

"I guess I am hungry," Meg admitted after taking the first mouthful. "I didn't realize it until now."

"I bet you didn't have lunch."

"You're right." Meg went on to explain what had happened at the station. "Would you believe he left me there?"

Kate smiled. "My nephew has a strange sense of humor sometimes."

"Then I found he had left a note with his receptionist instructing me to write copy for a new sponsor. If I wasn't so tired, I'd be tempted to kill him."

"I'm afraid I have more bad news for you," Kate added.

Meg glanced up. "What now?"

"Kyle left a message with me asking that you meet him at his house at six this evening. He wants to work up a more formal structure for your morning show."

"At his house?" Meg's voice rose slightly. "No way." Picking up the telephone on the nightstand, she glanced at Kate. "What's his number?"

As Kate spoke, Meg dialed. So he wanted her to go to his house to discuss business, did he? There was no way she would agree to meet him in so personal a setting. Had she been a man, he'd have taken her out for a drink someplace.

She gripped the receiver tightly when he answered. He was in for a rude awakening. "Kyle," she said firmly, "I have no intention of meeting you in your home at this hour. If you have business to discuss with me, I suggest you do it during business hours. If that can't be arranged, then we'll have to find a restaurant or coffee shop. Business should be discussed at a neutral meeting place. Your home is hardly that."

There was an ominous silence on the other end. "Are you finished?" he asked at length.

"Yes."

"Then let me explain something to you. My station is running on a shoestring budget. If you want to work for me, you'd better get used to working long hours. I'd take you someplace to have a drink, but it would neither be private nor very comfortable. My home, on the other hand, is both." He paused, then added, "So if you'll stop acting like a teenager and more like a business associate, I'd sure appreciate it."

His rebuff stung. Like her ex-husband, Kyle clearly didn't take challenges to his authority passively. He had gained the upper hand and made her feel extremely foolish. Well, she'd give in this time, but if he behaved toward her in anything but a professional manner, she'd leave—right after she punched him in the nose.

Chapter 5

MEG SAT AT Kyle's dining room table staring at the list of ideas he had typed up. It was incredible. His plans for the show were so rigidly formulated that they resembled plans for a full military offensive.

"I can't believe you," she said. "No show can be run this way. Look at this, for example." She pointed to the middle of the page. "Between nine-oh-five and nine-ten you want to run a community calendar. But by nine-eleven you're running a farmer's market report." She exhaled softly. "Kyle, this is too..."—she searched for the right word—"...dogmatic," she said at last.

"And what are your ideas?" he retorted a bit defensively. "I thought you'd at least have a few down on paper."

"I thought we'd discuss them like two mature people." She gave him a level stare. "After all, I'm an adult, and you closely resemble one."

"Cute."

"I thought so," she replied with an impish grin.

He chuckled softly. "All right. How about if I make some fresh coffee, and then, after we've had a chance to relax, we'll try to compromise."

"You realize," she ventured, following him into the small but orderly kitchen, "that the problem lies in our basic personality differences. What's completely natural for me is totally alien to you, and vice versa."

"Then we'd better figure out a way to get around those differences, because we have a show to do." He placed a plate of cookies on the counter and began pouring coffee into mugs.

"Chocolate-chip cookies," Meg acknowledged. "My favorite." She began to nibble on one. "The way I see it, your ideas are too rigid. Radio shows are normally divided into fifteen-minute segments, which is hard enough to handle. But you've got everything timed to the minute. That's an impossible demand. If you try to adhere to this schedule, you're going to drive yourself—and me—crazy."

"I tried flexibility today," he replied. "What could have become a Clean Up Cabezon Day turned into a car wash."

"So what? Tomorrow you can plug your idea again. Kyle, you won't sound relaxed on the air if you're trying to maintain a schedule that allots three minutes for this and five minutes for that."

"And what do you suggest?" He handed her a coffee mug that read THE BUCK STOPS HERE and pictured a reindeer butting his head against a brick wall.

"We want the audience to have fun listening to our show," she said. "Even more, we want them to take an active part in it. Let's get their attention by giving them something that's almost guaranteed to make them tune in each day."

"Like what?" He took a seat across the table from her.

She pursed her lips. "We could have trivia contests during the first fifteen minutes. Then we could have another segment in which the audience calls in and shares their best homemaker tips—everything from how to remove stubborn spots to how to make a fast meal for guests."

"I'll tell you what. Instead of just asking the audience, we'll compile our own homemaker tips, then ask the listeners to elaborate on them. Let's say we devote one of the shows to the theme of growing indoor flowering plants. We'll cover everything we can think of, then ask the folks what they've had the most success growing, and why. That way we're not just turning the show over to them. We're giving them information, educating them as much as we can on the particular subject, and asking them to share their insights."

She shrugged. "Sure, we could do that, but it'll take lots more work and research."

"But don't you think it'll be much better that way?" He began rapidly to scribble down notes. "As far as your trivia contest goes . . ." He paused, his eyebrows furrowing deeply. "We could place our focus on state and local government. We'll ask trivia questions concerning political issues and maybe even ask listeners to describe the duties associated with minor political posts. That way we can keep the public informed."

She saw immediate problems with his ideas, plus, his determination to modify everything she suggested was beginning to annoy her. "That's going to take hours of research!" she protested. "When are we supposed to do all this—in our spare time, between two and three in the morning?"

"It'll be more work, but think of what we can do for the public's awareness," he said enthusiastically. "It will be well worth the effort."

She walked to the small window over the kitchen sink and stared at the darkness outside. She had to force herself to calm down. Like her ex-husband, Kyle was trying to exercise control over every single one of her ideas. Couldn't he admit that her concepts were good, without trying to alter them until they became more his than hers?

Taking deep breaths, she tried to quiet her anger. "Kyle, if you already know what you want to do with the show, why did you ask me here?"

"I thought we were brainstorming," he countered. "Aren't you being overly sensitive? You should be happy that we spark ideas off each other so well."

"I guess so," she said hesitantly, staring vacantly across the room.

"You see, you've got practical experience on the air, and I'll admit you're great when it comes to getting the listeners to participate. But I know the people around here. I'm better attuned to their needs than you are."

"I suppose." Not wanting to face him, she walked to the sink and rinsed off the now empty cookie plate.

He came up from behind and placed his hands on her shoulders. "Why are you acting this way? There's got to be more to it than you're saying."

His touch sent a shiver up her spine. Without thinking, she turned to face him—and realized she'd made a mistake when she found herself mere inches away from him. Her back was touching the cabinet behind her. Unable to move away, she placed her palm on his chest, intending to push him gently back.

But he covered her hand with his own. "I'd like us to be friends, Meg," he said with warm sincerity.

"If you're really my friend," she said in a voice that sounded oddly strangled, "you'll move back a few steps. I think your sink is about to become permanently embedded in my spine."

His voice was like rich, dark velvet. "Is that the real reason?" he taunted gently. "Or could it be that my standing so close disturbs you?"

He stepped back anyway, and she moved away quickly. After refilling her coffee mug from a small pot on the stove, she wandered over to the adjoining den. An entertainment center ran along one wall. A dark leather sofa and chairs were arranged in the center of the room. An old Navajo rug lay over the back of the couch. The stone fireplace had an enormous tile hearth. Like Kyle himself, all the furnishings were ultra-masculine.

Spring Madness

"Tell me what's on your mind," he said from the doorway. "Why did you get so touchy when I modified your ideas? You don't seem like someone who thinks her ideas are too perfect to be improved on."

A hint of a smile tugged at the corners of her mouth. "No, that's your department."

"I'm not like that." Kyle crossed the room and sat down on the massive leather couch. "And you're changing the subject. Meg, we're going to be working closely together for the foreseeable future. It will make things easier for both of us if we understand each other. I realize you don't trust me very much, but I wish you'd tell me why you're so jumpy when we're alone together."

There was no way she could answer him. She wasn't about to admit that she found him incredibly appealing, that she was afraid those feelings would make her too eager to please him, and thus be easily controlled by him. "I'm not comfortable around you, Kyle. I'm afraid that if I relax and let my guard down, we'll be tempted to try and learn too much about each other. Business relationships work better when there's an emotional distance built in."

"You've never been one to play by the rules. Why now?" he countered smoothly. "If you never let me get past the casual acquaintance stage, we're going to spend the rest of this year playing twenty questions—you in the role of the young resistance leader who's vowed never to divulge any information except her name, rank, and serial number."

Meg laughed. "You're certainly persistent and persuasive. I'll tell you what. I'll make a deal with you. Ask me whatever you want, and I'll try to answer as honestly as I can. Afterward it'll be my turn to ask the questions."

"That sounds ominous."

"Hey, fair's fair."

"All right," he conceded with a grin. "Tell me why you were so touchy about having your ideas modified."

"Back to that again, are we?"

"You never answered me."

"All right." She settled deep into the cushions. "I guess it all dates back to when I was married to Mike Randall. I met him during my junior year at college. He was the captain of the football team and the handsomest man I'd ever seen. I fell head over heels in love with him. When he asked me to marry him a year later, I was ecstatic. I knew Mike was demanding, but I thought that once we were married, we'd learn to adapt to each other and everything would be fine." She took a deep breath. "Of course, it wasn't. As time went by I began to resent the fact that he expected me always to place my needs and wants second to his. He wanted to be the focal point of my life. He didn't want me to become involved with anything that didn't directly involve him. I quit college at the start of my senior year because he was so adamant about it. He claimed I was so busy studying that I never had enough time to be a wife. It became quite an issue, so I finally capitulated and quit.

"That got to be a pattern for us," Meg went on. "We'd fight. He'd twist my words around, make me feel guilty when I tried to stand up for myself, and in the end, I'd give in."

"How long did that go on?" Kyle asked quietly.

"It took two years for our marriage to self-destruct. I needed a life of my own. I couldn't stay home forever, living out my life through him. You see, Kyle, during those two years I had to live with a man who constantly put down my ideas as worthless. Whenever he had a problem at his lumber store, I'd try to help. Most of the time he completely brushed aside my suggestions. But if he was forced to accept one of my ideas because he couldn't think of anything better, he'd change it until I hardly recognized it as my own. That way he could claim that my contribution had been negligible."

"Now I know why you got angry when we were brainstorming." Kyle clasped her hand tenderly between both of his. "I'm not like your ex-husband, Meg. As far as

I'm concerned, we're a team. We'll be equally infamous," he added roguishly.

She chuckled, then grew serious. "I'll try to stop being so sensitive."

"I have only one question. If you thought Mike was deliberately trying to control you by making you feel guilty, why did you continue to let him do it?"

"Mike knew how much I loved him, and he used my feelings against me. When I really care for someone, I instinctively want to please them. That's my Achilles' heel." She instantly regretted admitting so much to him. "But enough about me. Let's talk about you for a change."

"What would you like to know?"

"Do you have any brothers or sisters? Does your family live here in town?"

"My parents moved to Texas years ago, and my brother, who works for the Diplomatic Corps, is in Madrid right now."

"Do you miss them?"

He nodded. "I miss my brother, Bill, most of all, but we talk all the time. Our phone bills are an absolute disaster." He chuckled. "Still, Bill and I like to keep in touch."

"Are you the older brother?"

Kyle shook his head. "Bill is. You know, it's really strange that we ended up being so close because I remember always being in an unofficial competition with him. I felt pressured to become as successful as he was. That's why I accepted the job with the oil company and worked so hard to make it to the top."

"It must have taken a great deal of courage to walk away from your job and start your own radio station."

"It was, and still is, a risk. I've sunk every penny I saved into this, and then I borrowed an enormous sum so I could get off to a good start. So far, KHAY's losing more money than it takes in, and I can't sustain that loss for very long. I truly believe, though, that if I can hang in there for just a little while longer, I'll be able to break even, then start making a profit. Vultures like Monica

Hanrahan, however, are the bane of my existence."

"At least you know where you can find a buyer if you have to."

"I hate even to consider the possibility." Kyle stretched out his legs and continued thoughtfully: "This radio station stands for everything I've ever wanted. I'm not about to lose it without one whale of a fight."

"Have you ever been married, Kyle?"

He shook his head. "My life's hardly been monastic, Meg, but as for a special person..."—he pursed his lips—"...there's only been one."

"What was she like?" she asked hesitantly, torn between the desire to know more about him and a reluctance to bring back memories of a woman who had figured so prominently in his past.

"Anna was unique," he said in a faraway tone. "There was something incredibly vibrant about her. She was an engineer for the oil company where I worked. At first I thought she was everything I had ever wanted in a woman, but slowly I began to see another side of her. She cared more for money and status than she did for anything else in life—including me. When she was offered a prestigious overseas post with the company, she took it. I couldn't blame her, really. It was everything she had been working for. Stationed in a politically volatile section of the Middle East, she'd encounter plenty of excitement, plus she'd be earning two to three times what she had in the States." Kyle's jaw tightened. "Anna would never have been content with an ordinary life. It was best that we separated when we did. Sometimes love alone just isn't enough."

"Only if there isn't enough love," Meg countered.

"Now who's playing with words?" He smiled ruefully.

"It's true. In my case what originally drew me to Mike was a physical attraction. That overshadowed everything else to the extent that I dismissed character traits I knew would be difficult to deal with. Had my love been based on something more substantial, it might also have been deep enough to allow me to accept him as he was."

"So you believe that love conquers all?"

"If the love is genuine, it gives you the drive to surmount whatever obstacles stand in the way."

"I wouldn't have thought it, but you're not only a romantic, you're also an idealist."

"Perhaps." The topic was suddenly making her feel very uneasy. "Hey, we were supposed to be talking about you."

He laughed. "So we were."

"Do you still miss Anna?" Meg felt compelled to ask.

"No. After she left I decided it was time I started pursuing my own goals. In a way she was a catalyst for me. I saw that she was attaining what she had always wanted, and I started thinking of myself and what would make me happy. About a year after she left I decided to come back to Cabezon."

"And now that you have your own radio station, what's next?"

"Making it a success," he countered good-naturedly. "And, of course, I don't plan to spend the rest of my life as a bachelor. I'm not actively looking for a wife, but I'm not closed to the possibility either."

"With me it's just the opposite," she replied, feeling uneasy. She avoided his eyes and toyed with her ring. "I've had my fill of marriage. At first I thought being single was painfully lonesome. Then I stopped thinking of myself as all alone, and started thinking of myself as on my own. Nowadays I'm enjoying the freedom. Being single means that I answer only to myself. There's a great deal of satisfaction in knowing that I'm completely responsible for what becomes of me."

"I used to think the same thing," he answered, "so I know what you mean. Just make sure being single doesn't become an obsession with you. Life is meant for couples."

"I don't think so," she replied resolutely.

"Eating dinner alone, going to movies alone, and in general doing everything with only yourself for company can be rough sometimes. I won't argue against the obvious advantages, but being single also has its disadvantages. Don't blind yourself to them."

The second she met his eyes, she knew she had made a mistake. The sexual tension between them sprang to life. Despite her valiant words about her need for freedom, another side of her craved the security and warmth of his embrace. Remembering the feel of his lips on hers, she unconsciously flicked her tongue over her lips.

"Don't do that," he warned. "You're tempting enough as is."

She realized what he meant almost instantly. "I'm sorry. I..." She stopped, suddenly breathless.

"Yes, I know," he said in response to her unasked question. "Our feelings are growing, and with them our need for each other."

She felt as if a thousand tiny electric currents were flitting across her body. "No. I can't allow myself to think in those terms. I don't want to repeat the past. Physical attraction only brings trouble. My marriage to Mike was a perfect example of that."

"What's happening between us is more than physical, Meg. I know you sense that as well as I do," he said, edging closer to her. His arm came to rest across her shoulders. His thumb drew lazy circles on the nape of her neck.

She felt her resistance melting. The realization of how badly she wanted him frightened her into action. Instinctively she jumped to her feet.

He looked up in surprise. "Are you that scared of your own feelings, Meg, or do I threaten you?"

"I don't know what you're talking about, Kyle," she denied. "I just feel energetic right now. Why don't we get back to work?"

He gave in gallantly. "All right." He patted the cushion beside him. "Come back here, and we'll see if we can come up with some more ideas for our show."

If she sat beside him, she knew they wouldn't talk business. The prudent course of action would be to bid him good-night, and go home. But she didn't want to leave—not just yet. "Can we step outside in your backyard and get some fresh air?" she suggested.

"Sure." He opened the sliding-glass door. A soft breeze sighed through the cottonwood trees in the garden. Tiny insects flitted past them as they strolled peacefully under the moonlit sky.

"You're so near me, yet so far," Kyle murmured, reaching for her hand.

At first she wanted to refuse the gesture, but his grasp was warm, firm, and comforting. She turned to look at him, spellbound by a heavenly charm. Her feelings were weaving a trap around her, and the worst part was that she didn't want to escape.

He cupped her face tenderly, his thumb gently caressing her cheek. "You make me want you," he said simply, yet the reverberations of his tone worked their way to her very core.

Her heart did somersaults as she surrendered to the sweet weakness that invaded her. "You shouldn't say things like that," she managed to say, making one last attempt to resist the need he had awakened within her.

He pulled her toward him and held her tightly against him. "Don't push me away, Meg. Let me hold you, even if just for a minute," he ordered softly.

She meant to refuse, but somehow the words became lodged in her throat. "You want me because I'm a challenge to you," she whispered.

"I want you because you're a very desirable woman," he insisted softly. "There's a side of you that needs someone to soothe away the hurt."

A feverish want surged through her in dizzying waves. Her body tingled expectantly. She longed to surrender, yet she could not. Her imagination taunted her unmercifully. The thought of lying naked with Kyle fired her senses. Only the certain knowledge that pursuing the dictates of her body would exact too high a price stopped her from going further.

Pushing him away became a test of her resolve as she struggled to vanquish the primitive side of her that longed for his touch. "Coming out here was a bad idea," she said. "Let's go back inside and finish our business discussion."

"Don't run away," he said, gently grasping her arm.

In the dim light his eyes looked like two deep pools of turbulent water as they smoldered with burning passion.

The desire she saw there kindled her own, and in that instant she knew he would kiss her and that she'd do nothing to stop him.

He must have sensed her thoughts. As his lips descended, Meg caught a glimpse of his victorious smile.

The sensations that flooded over her blocked out everything except the wonderful hard feel of him pressing against her. Her hands traveled over his smoothly muscled shoulders. Kyle's arms tightened about her in response. His questing tongue sought hers as he deepened the kiss. Driven by relentless male hunger, he explored the warm recesses beyond her parted lips with a boldness that left her quivering in his arms.

Tearing her mouth from his, she moaned softly. "Kyle, please don't."

He stroked her hair tenderly, and for an instant she yielded, burying herself in the warmth of his embrace. It would be so easy...

"We need time to get to know each other," he whispered, tightening his hold on her. "Once we do, working together will be a lot easier."

His statement reached into her mind, bringing back painful memories of her marriage to Mike. Was Kyle hoping that by mastering her senses with his touch, she'd also bend to his will in every other respect? The thought angered her.

Very deliberately she moved away from him. "Please leave me alone," she said. "If you think you can seduce me into being more cooperative at work, then you'd better forget it. It won't work."

As she said the words, she knew that was her biggest fear of all. "I will not be pressured into anything, Kyle.

If you want someone who'll approve of everything you do or say, then you've picked the wrong person."

He stared at her in surprise. "Is it so hard to accept that all I want is the chance to enjoy your company?"

She strode back inside the house. "It's the other things you want that worry me," she retorted, then paused. "Kyle," she said finally, "I think it's time I went home. I need a chance to be alone and think."

He didn't stop her when she picked up her purse from the couch and walked to the door. Resisting the temptation to glance back, she left the house, got into her car, and drove home.

Chapter 6

MEG LAY IN bed, fully clothed, and stared at the ceiling. Why did men have to complicate everything! Her thoughts were in such a jumble. She felt as if she'd been given a gift certificate to the best ice-cream parlor in the world just when she most needed to go on a diet. She had to keep Kyle at an emotional distance if she was going to have any peace of mind at all! Yet, that was becoming increasingly difficult with each passing day.

Hearing someone knock on her door, she sat up abruptly. "Yes?" she called. Maybe Kyle had come to say he was sorry.

"It's Kate, dear. I thought you might like a cup of herb tea before going to sleep."

Her heart sank. Reluctantly getting out of bed, she opened the door. "Hi," she said, stepping aside in a silent invitation for Kate to enter.

"I heard you come in, and when you didn't even stop by the kitchen to say hello, I figured something must have upset you," Kate explained.

"It's nothing," Meg hedged.

Kate set the small tray containing a china teapot and a plate of cookies on the bedside table. "Well, in any case, I do believe that a little snack before bedtime can make anyone feel better. The cookies are fresh, too. I baked them only a few hours ago."

Meg smiled. "Kate, I really appreciate your kindness, but you shouldn't have gone to all this trouble."

"It's no trouble." She smiled sheepishly. "In all honesty, it's nice to have someone to fuss over."

Although Meg wasn't the least bit hungry, she nibbled absentmindedly on a cookie. "You know, I'm glad Kyle told me you were looking for a boarder. I thought that moving out here, knowing no one, would be one of the hardest things I'd ever done. But you've made it so easy."

"It's good for me, too, Meg. I'm used to living alone, but it's much more pleasant to have company."

"I agree." She accepted the cup of tea Kate held out.

"You're good for Kyle, too," Kate said after a brief silence.

Noting that Kate had avoided looking at her as she made the statement, Meg gave the elderly woman a long, speculative glance. "You wouldn't be trying to matchmake, would you?" she said finally.

Kate sighed. "I guess I'm not very good at being surreptitious."

"You're absolutely rotten at it," Meg agreed, smiling.

"Let me just say this, then." She looked directly at Meg. "I think you two bring out the best in each other, both over the radio and in person. There's something special about you two as a team. Be patient with him and with yourself, and then"—she winked—"consider the possibilities."

"Kate, I'm not looking for a husband. I was married once and that was enough."

"Kyle's young and alone, and so are you. Don't waste your youth. This is a time when you should be making memories that will last a lifetime. When you get to be my age, you'll see how important it is to be able to look

Spring Madness

back and know you never ran away from the best life has to offer simply because you were too afraid to take risks. When my husband died, I thought that loving carried too high a price. I was wrong. It carried a price, yes, but what we shared was so special that those memories will see me through the rest of my life. As long as he's in here"—she pointed to her heart—"he'll never be far away."

"People dream of finding a love like the one you had," Meg replied thoughtfully, "but relationships like that are rare these days."

"Fiddlesticks!" Kate exclaimed with a deprecating wave of her hand. "It's just that people aren't willing to give enough of themselves to make it happen." She gently patted Meg's hand and stood up. "I'm starting to preach to you, and I know how young people hate that." She paused at the door. "Do think about what I've said, Meg."

Before Meg had a chance to answer, Kate was gone.

For several minutes Meg leaned against her pillows, lost in thought. Kate meant well, and a lot of what she had said made sense. Still, to "give of herself," as Kate had put it, meant leaving herself vulnerable. That type of trust came easily to people who had yet to suffer the pain of disillusionment and betrayal, but she wasn't sure she had the capacity to be that open with anyone. Divorce always left scars, and in her case they seemed to be permanent.

Meg awoke to a strange tapping sound. She lay still for several seconds, trying to determine the source. Just as she was about to drop off to sleep again, she heard a light thump against her windowpane. Wide awake now, she tossed the covers aside, parted the curtains, and peered out the open window.

In the moonlight she could see Kyle below. "I need to talk to you," he called, "but I don't want to wake up Aunt Kate."

"You don't want to wake *her* up!" Meg exclaimed. "What about waking *me* up? Oh, all right," she suddenly relented. "I'll meet you downstairs."

Bedecked in furry slippers and a robe, she opened the front door for him. "It's one in the morning, Kyle," she whispered. "You'd better have an excellent reason for waking me up at this hour."

"I kept thinking of what happened tonight and I just couldn't sleep," he said. "I really think it's important that we resolve what's bothering you. Also, I honestly would like to know what you think of my proposed program log before we go on the air tomorrow."

"You're not considering going over the format for our show *now*, are you?" She folded her arms across her chest.

He smiled roguishly. "By the time we broadcast tomorrow, I want to have a clear picture of what we're doing."

"Have a heart, will you?" She glanced at her wristwatch. "We only have a few more hours of sleep time left."

"Do you approve of the program segments we've thought of so far for the show?"

"Not completely, but if agreeing to them will get you to leave so I can go back to sleep, I'm willing to give them a try."

"All right." He smiled. "You look beautiful right now, you know."

Suddenly self-conscious about her appearance, she wrapped her robe tightly around her, her fists curled around the fabric. "Will you please go home?"

"Very few women look as beautiful as you do without any makeup on," he said, ignoring her remark.

She groaned. "Kyle."

"By the way, you were wrong about me." His eyes burned with hunger as they sizzled down the length of her. "I'd never try to coerce you into becoming something you're not—for example, docile." He gave her a teasing wink.

"You're in no immediate danger of that," she retorted.

Spring Madness

Kyle laughed. "I didn't think I was. I just wanted you to know where I stand."

"What the heck is so funny?" she countered, pursing her lips. "You make me feel as if my sole purpose in life is to act as comic relief!"

He kissed her impulsively on the cheek. "You make me laugh, Meg. That's not so bad, is it?"

"That depends. Are you laughing at me, with me, or in spite of me?"

"I'm laughing because you're delightful." He reached for her hand and gave it a tender squeeze. "Good night, my sweet. See you later."

Meg fought the urge to slam the door behind him. Kyle Rager was the most infuriating man in the world, yet something about him made her feel more vibrantly feminine than she ever had before.

Their new program managed to incorporate both Meg's need for flexibility and Kyle's need for structure. The various segments, from the trivia contests to the helpful household tips, quickly began to acquire a loyal following. Their format was only four days old when, judging by the increased number of telephone calls to the station, it was deemed a success.

Meg sat on the carpeted floor in Kyle's office, leafing through volumes of *Who's Who*. "The idea you had earlier this morning about honoring Americans whose contributions to society were above and beyond the call of duty is great in theory, but it's a headache in practice," she said. "How the heck am I even supposed to *find* these people, let alone write profiles on them? In order to locate them, I have to know all about them—and how can I know all about them if I can't find them?"

"Aren't you glad I've given you this terrific opportunity to impress me with your resourcefulness?" Kyle shot back good-naturedly. "Besides, my job isn't easy either. I've got to write an entertaining script on the care and feeding of goats."

"Goats?" She looked up, amused. "Are you kidding?"

"No. They're really popular around here. In fact, there's a statewide goat show the weekend after next."

"A goat show?" she asked incredulously. "Are you sure you've got that right?"

"Sure." He shrugged. "From what I've found out so far, African pygmy goats are really popular. The larger breeds are used for everything from dairy animals to companions for horses."

"On second thought, I'll stick with *Who's Who*," Meg said. "I'd rather try to find a contemporary American hero than compile a list of enthralling reasons for owning a goat."

She had just started to look through the newspaper when a paper airplane collided with her nose and landed with a soft *thwack!* in front of her. "You've just been dive-bombed," Kyle explained.

"And you need a psychiatrist."

She started to say more, but at that instant Monica Hanrahan strolled into Kyle's office. Wearing an elegant burgundy silk blouse and a black linen skirt, she exuded the undefinable look of authority and assurance that came from having power and money.

Monica glanced down at Meg with an expression of haughty contempt. "Really, dear, you shouldn't let Kyle work you like a slave. Don't you at least merit a chair and desk?"

Meg chuckled softly, darting a quick look at Kyle.

He rolled his eyes. "Monica, let me tell you about a quaint custom called knocking. One does it before entering another person's room."

"And miss the opportunity to drive you crazy?" She flashed a mocking smile. "Not on your life."

"To what do we owe the displeasure of your visit?" Kyle countered.

"I wanted to tell you not to get your hopes up too high. Your station is showing signs of life, but in the end can't compete with KLUV. You simply haven't got the resources." Monica gave him a catlike smile and

Spring Madness

made herself comfortable on a corner of his desk. "But I must say the competition, such as it is, is making things a little more lively."

"I still don't know what you're doing here, Monica," Kyle said.

"I want you to know I appreciate the gallant effort you're making to stay in business. I'll try to remember that when it's time to buy you out."

Kyle laughed. "Sure you will. And you'll be glad to pay me exactly what KHAY's worth—as long as I'm willing to accept payment in T-shirts with your name on them, right?"

Monica chuckled. "So you do admit that sooner or later KHAY will be mine."

"I was trying to make a different point, my greedy friend." Kyle ushered her politely to the door. "And now, if you're finished, Meg and I have a lot of work to do."

After giving Meg a tiny wave, Monica leaned toward Kyle and kissed him on the cheek. "I can't wait until you're working for me," she said seductively.

Before Kyle could react, Monica strolled away.

"The gall of that woman!" He grimaced. "I think I'd rather be kissed by a cobra."

"There are worse fates than catching the interest of a beautiful woman," Meg observed.

"Monica Hanrahan is not a beautiful woman. She's a barracuda in drag."

Meg laughed. "Aw, poor baby," she teased. "Shall I kiss it and make it better?"

He gave her a lazy smile. "Sure can, my sweet."

Without warning he swept her into his arms. She was trying to recapture her balance, her hands splayed against his chest, when his lips came crashing down over hers. Kyle feasted on her mouth, deepening the kiss. Desire tore at her with relentless insistence, and she fought a wild longing to go someplace where they'd be safe from interruptions, and hidden from prying eyes.

"No," she said at length. "That's enough, Kyle. We're playing with fire. Although I realize that, to you, that just adds to the thrill, I'm much too conservative to play your game."

"You're conservative and I'm the daring one?" He stared at her in disbelief. "When did we switch roles?"

Without answering, she returned to her place on the floor and resumed working. "If Monica's going to launch an offensive," she said at last, "we'd better come up with an idea that will keep our audience faithful."

He chuckled at her obvious attempt to change the subject. "What do you have in mind?"

"How about a contest with a prize?"

"We can't afford it."

"It doesn't have to cost a lot of money. What we need is something that will get our listeners involved. A game of sorts."

He pursed his lips. "You might have a point there. How about a treasure hunt?"

"That's a great idea!"

"The problem is: What do we use as a treasure?"

Meg concentrated. "We need a prize that will tie in to the station and act as advertising for KHAY. That way, we'll be getting twice as much for our efforts."

"Now, if we could only figure out what that could be, we'd have it made."

For several minutes neither one said anything. Meg began to pace around the room. "To be consistent with your philosophy," she began, "it has to be something that shows that KHAY cares for the community. Since we can't really afford something terribly expensive, the thought behind it has to evoke just the right sentiment."

"How about burying T-shirts with the logo 'KHAY Loves New Mexico'?" he suggested. "We could even put on one of those little hearts instead of spelling out the word *love*."

"That's great, except for two things. First, what size T-shirts would you bury? And when people found out that the station's treasure was only a T-shirt, don't you think that both you, and the station, would look cheap?"

Spring Madness 79

"I prefer to think of it as frugal." He crossed his arms over his chest.

"You're not talking frugal, Kyle. You're talking *cheap*."

He shrugged. "Okay. So come up with a better idea."

She began pacing again. "I think you were on the right track when you thought of a heart." She stopped abruptly and faced him. "How about buying a solid gold heart and having it engraved with 'KHAY always cares'? We could start plugging the contest as KHAY's treasure hunt—brought especially to you from the station with the heart of gold."

"*Gold* heart? That's going to cost a fortune!"

"So make it a small one and encase it in a beautiful velvet box. Then we'll bury it someplace."

"You mean about the size of a charm or a pendant?"

"That's the idea," she replied enthusiastically.

He nodded. "I like it. In fact, I think it's close to being brilliant."

"Close to?"

"Had it been my idea, it would have been brilliant," he teased, "but since it was yours, naturally I have to modify my compliment. I wouldn't want success to go to your head."

"God forbid!" she countered with mock horror.

"Where shall we bury it?"

"This is your town, so I'll leave that to you." She bit her lip. "Wait, I just had a terrific idea. It's rather sinister, though."

"Let's hear it."

"We'll bury it right underneath KLUV's sign in front of Monica Hanrahan's station! Nobody would accidentally find it *there!*"

Kyle laughed so hard that he had to lean against his desk for support. "I love it. It's truly Machiavellian. That, my beautiful partner, *is* a brilliant idea."

"Praise at last!"

"You realize that if she catches us, she'll have us

executed at dawn," Kyle cautioned.

"Then it looks like we'll have to do the foul deed in the dead of night," Meg countered.

He reached out and lightly caressed her cheek. "Lady, I really like you."

Though his touch sent an unexpected tremor through her body, she didn't draw away. "Since we're partners, that's the way it should be," she replied unsteadily.

Chapter 7

TWO DAYS LATER Meg accompanied Kyle on an afternoon shopping trip in search of just the right gold heart. It was late evening by the time they found exactly what they were looking for.

Meg stared at the two delicately handcrafted hearts. "They're beautiful."

"They're the only two of their kind," the goldsmith informed them, "but I can sell them to you either separately or as a set."

Meg glanced at Kyle. "One of these would be perfect for what we want." She picked up one of the tiny pendants. "I only wish I had the money to buy the other one," she added sadly.

Kyle took the heart from her and glanced up at the goldsmith. "We'll need to have it engraved."

"I can do it right now, while you wait, if you'd like," he offered.

Kyle accepted gratefully.

Meg and Kyle waited patiently while the goldsmith

went about his task of engraving the pendant.

On their return trip to Cabezon Meg fingered the delicate pendant. "I envy whoever finds it," she murmured.

Kyle glanced over at her. His eyes softened with a tender warmth that caused her pulse to leap. As his gaze dropped to the heart resting delicately in the palm of her hand, he squeezed her arm gently. "You know what? I just had a great idea. If you're not too tired when we get back, why don't we sneak out to KLUV and bury it tonight?"

Meg chuckled. "We might as well; otherwise, I might be tempted to abscond with our treasure."

Kyle just winked.

Shortly after eleven that evening Meg walked downstairs, dressed completely in black and feeling like a cat burglar. Kyle had already arrived and was busy consuming Kate's chocolate-chip cookies.

"You look appropriately sinister," he said, eyeing with approval Meg's black slacks and black turtleneck sweater.

"Look who's talking," she replied, giving his charcoal-colored sweat shirt and dark parachute pants a cursory glance. "You look like you're ready to invade Normandy Beach."

"In a way we are," he replied, grinning.

"You're right," she said, and laughed. "You do realize that Monica is going to want to boil us in oil for this."

"Are you *sure* you want to bury the treasure beside KLUV's outdoor sign?" Kate asked seriously. "Monica might have you arrested for vandalism or, at the very least, trespassing, if she catches you digging in her lawn." She removed a sheet of freshly baked cookies from the oven.

"That woman's been a thorn in my side for a long time," Kyle said. "I can't tell you how glad I am to have a chance to pay her back in kind."

"Well." Meg raised a glass of milk in a toast. "Here's to two future jailbirds."

Kyle shook his head. "Here's to not getting caught," he amended.

"Amen to that."

"Are you ready for our great adventure?" he asked, taking one last cookie from the plate Kate had set out.

"As much as I'll ever be."

Kate clucked in disapproval. "You two be careful, and remember to call me if you need someone to bail you out of jail."

Meg kissed her lightly on the cheek. "We'll be careful, I promise." She gave Kyle a teasing glance and added, "And don't worry. If we get caught, I'll blame it all on Kyle. You won't lose your boarder."

Kate feigned great relief. "In that case I won't worry about a thing."

"Thanks a lot, Aunt Kate," Kyle protested.

Meg strode past him to the door. "Don't give the lady a hard time. She obviously knows who's indispensable and who's not."

Thirty minutes later Kyle parked his sedan about a block away from KLUV. "It'll be better if we sneak up on foot," he explained. "We'll have to work fast, though. Their midnight disk jockey is inside, and a security patrol car makes its rounds periodically."

Careful to stay in the shadows, Kyle and Meg worked their way down the boulevard, hurrying from tree to bush. Taking cover behind a sculptured hedge, they crouched in wait as a car drove by. KLUV's large station sign stood on the landscaped area in front of their facility, supported by two wooden posts. The glow of a distant streetlight cast a shadow of the sign across the lawn.

Just as Meg was about to speak, she heard a noise. She froze, then whispered to Kyle, "Don't move. Somebody is behind us."

Noiselessly they lowered themselves to the ground and remained motionless. Soft shuffling footsteps approached from the rear of the leaf-littered grass. The sound of heavy breathing made Meg suddenly afraid. Anxiously she turned to look at Kyle, who slid his arm around her in a comforting gesture. Just then a large bulldog appeared in front of them, panting loudly in the warm evening. The animal stopped and stared curiously at their two huddled figures.

Kyle's hushed laughter was met with a stony glare from Meg. "This never happened to James Bond," she mumbled as she reached out to pet the dog.

The animal growled a warning, then moved on, continuing his midnight prowl. Soon all was quiet again.

"That'll teach you to be more choosy picking your friends," Kyle whispered. "Let's get back to business. Do you have that little hand shovel we brought?"

"Sure do." She handed it to him. "I'll wait here while you dig."

"Nothing doing," he shot back. "We're in this together."

"Why should we both get caught?"

"Equal rights, equal risks. Besides, it was your idea."

"Which you'll be glad to tell the cops once we're arrested," she grumpily predicted.

"Of course." Still crouching, he inched forward and peered around. "Okay, coast's clear. Let's get to it."

Meg held a tiny flashlight as Kyle cut out a square of turf. He dug a hole deep enough to cover the small box, which they'd wrapped in foil, then replaced the grass. With meticulous care he pressed the turf down carefully so that the excavation wouldn't show. "Let's get out of here," he whispered harshly as he finished.

At that instant Meg heard the radio station's side door open, then slam shut. Monica's voice could be heard over the stillness of the evening. "I want you to continue playing the oldies at night. We seem to have had a very favorable response to our Solid Gold Hour."

Meg inhaled sharply. "We've got to get out of here," she said softly.

"This way." Kyle pulled her down onto the grass. Forcing her to crawl on all fours, he led the way to cover.

Spring Madness 85

They waited behind the shelter of a cluster of cacti.

Monica strolled past them, just inches away from their hiding place. Just when Meg was about to breathe a sigh of relief, Monica stopped.

For what seemed like an eternity she searched in her purse, then pulled out a cigarette and lit it.

Meg held her breath. After a few moments Monica continued down the path, then entered her car and drove away. "Phew! That was close!" Meg exclaimed.

"First one bulldog, then another," Kyle joked. "I should have expected this. Monica's a workaholic, and the station's her pet project. We're lucky she didn't spot us."

Still avoiding the sidewalk and staying well in the shadows, but feeling less tense, they headed back to Kyle's car. Suddenly Meg spotted a bright searchlight sweeping over the shop fronts and bushes toward which they were walking. The intense beam of light glaringly exposed everything it touched.

Kyle muttered an oath. The spotlight, standard equipment on most police vehicles, was moving in their direction. "There's the patrol car!" he said. "They'll catch us for sure with that spotlight."

Reacting quickly, he grabbed Meg's waist and pulled her into his arms, letting the shovel he'd been holding drop to the grass.

"What the—"

"Quiet," he whispered in her ear. "Let the cop think we're just two lovers out for a moonlight stroll."

As the light's beam approached, he tangled his hand in her thick hair, and pulled her head back to meet his descending lips. His mouth moved over hers, deliberately teasing her lips with sensual promise. As his tongue slipped into the intimate warmth of her, she moaned softly.

Even though her eyes were closed, she knew when the bright light flooded over them. She heard a faint chuckle in the distance. Then a voice called out, "Atta way, Kyle!"

Meg almost choked. She tried to pull away, but Kyle

held her steady, his lips imprisoning hers in a thoroughly audacious kiss. She heard the patrol car drive past. When all was silent once again, Kyle released her.

Squaring her shoulders, she glared at him. "'Atta boy, Kyle'?" she said, mimicking the police officer. "You should have let me toss the shovel at him."

"That's called assault, and you'd have landed in jail," Kyle said good-naturedly. "Besides, John is a friend of mine."

"You *know* the officer on this beat?"

"Of course. I grew up a block away from him."

"Then why were you acting as if we were about to be arrested? If he's your friend, wouldn't he have known you weren't a thief casing the place?"

"Sure."

"Then you didn't need to kiss me after all. It was just a trick," she challenged, indignant at having been manipulated.

"Of course." Kyle opened the car door on the passenger's side. "I wanted to kiss you, and that seemed like a perfect opportunity."

Meg wasn't speechless for long. "You rotten, no-good, son of a toad! How dare you take advantage of me! Who do you think you are?"

"Your partner in crime, of course," he answered playfully. "And you know what they say about honor among thieves."

Ten days passed. Although KHAY's jocks had been instructed to read Meg and Kyle's clues once an hour, none of their listeners had found the gold heart. The promotion was going well. It had already continued longer than they'd originally predicted, and from all indications their listening audience was growing.

Meg prepared to read the latest clue over the air. She and Kyle had worked hours trying to come up with a revealing tip that would ensure their prize was found soon, when public attention was at its peak. "Now, ladies

Spring Madness

and gentlemen," she said, "listen carefully, and we're sure to find our winner today:

> Beneath the darkened sign of love,
> Our heart is hidden from above,
> Just for one who comes to find,
> A caring gift we've left behind."

After switching on an ad and turning down the microphones, Meg gave Kyle a speculative look. "What do you think? Shall we instruct our photographer, that poor little gal who's been hiding in the van across from KLUV all week, to take a candid photograph of Monica when she finds out about our heinous deed?"

Kyle laughed. "What an inspired idea!" He gave her shoulder an affectionate squeeze. "Lady, there are times when I wonder what I ever did without you."

For a moment Meg was lost for an answer. The notion that Kyle might return what she was feeling for him made it harder to hide her interest in him. She knew that emotionally she was walking on thin ice. The elusive promise of what could be between them threatened to break apart the last vestiges of her self-control.

She needed a diversion, a gambit that would redirect her thoughts and diffuse the tension. She switched on the microphone. "Ladies and gentlemen, I want you to know that Kyle has just admitted that he'd be lost without me," she announced.

Kyle began to choke, but covered it up by clearing his throat. "Not quite," he said. "It's more like I don't know what to do *with* you."

"Taking it back, are you?" she teased. "I wonder if I can sue for breach of promise."

"I wonder if I can get a new partner," he countered.

As soon as they returned to their musical program, Kyle picked up the telephone. "I'd give anything to get a photo of Monica's face when she finds out where the heart is hidden. She's going to be fuming!"

"And I bet that'll make your day," Meg said with a grin.

Spotting the red light indicating an incoming call, Kyle picked up the receiver, then switched the communication over to the box on the console. "KHAY, the station with the heart of gold. This is Kyle Rager. Can I help you?"

"You swine!" Monica's voice was amplified in the booth. "You've got a heck of a lot of nerve burying *your* promotional trinket under *my* sign."

Kyle's eyes sparkled with devilish amusement. "Wait a minute, Monica. Are you saying that *you* found it? What were you doing looking for it in the first place?"

"I make it my business to know what your station is up to. Your childish clues were so idiotically simple that I began to get suspicious. I decided to check them out, and of course I found the heart. Your little trinket now belongs to me."

"May I quote you as saying that any idiot could find the heart, and you proved it?" Kyle retorted.

"Only if you want to hear from my lawyer." Monica's anger was obviously escalating. "And one more thing. Your stupid photographer has enough shots of me digging it up, too! If you print them, Kyle Rager, I swear I'll have your head."

Kyle let out more whoops of laughter. "I'm not only going to print them, I'll have them distributed from every street corner!" he declared.

Meg chuckled. "Ask her if she wants to go on the air as our winner."

"Did you hear that?" He repeated the question.

Monica's voice rose shrilly. "You want war, do you? Well, you've got it, buddy boy. No more playing nice. I'm going to wipe that little radio station of yours clear off the map."

As the sound of the dial tone echoed in their headsets, Kyle and Meg continued to laugh.

"And there you have it. Another satisfied winner," Meg teased. "Shall we announce the news over the air?"

Spring Madness   89

"You bet. In fact, I think I'll do the honors myself."

The news captured Cabezon by surprise. The KHAY telephone lines began to ring frantically as people called in to share their amusement.

It was close to noon by the time Meg and Kyle were finally free to take a break. "I'm starving," Meg said over the loud rumbling in her stomach. "Why don't you ask me out to lunch?"

"I have a better idea. Why don't you take me?"

"If I did," she ventured cautiously, "would I have to pick up the tab?"

"Most definitely."

"Then it's no deal," she said with feigned sorrow. "You see, my boss is a real tightwad. He hardly pays me enough to feed myself, let alone him, too."

He pretended to mull over the idea of taking her out to lunch. "If I feed you, will you follow me home so I can keep you?"

"You've got it all wrong," she countered smoothly. "That works only with puppies."

"I'll tell you what. I'll feed you if you write the next set of trivia questions."

"All right. But if I write the questions, will you log the music program for this week?"

He sighed. "Forget it. I'll pay for the lunch if you'll stop negotiating."

"Hey, I didn't start this. You did."

"Likely excuse," he teased.

Enjoying the breeze and the bright sunshine, they walked to a small café a block from the station.

"I'd better warn you," Kyle said. "Their Mexican dishes are really hot, so be careful what you order if you don't want to feel as if you're going up in flames."

The waitress greeted them warmly. "Hi! We were wondering when you two were going to stop by. We always listen to your show. You guys make a perfect team."

"Thanks," Meg replied, feeling like a celebrity.

"If I put you two in the middle of the room, you won't get enough privacy even to finish lunch," she said in a conspiratorial whisper, "so why don't I seat you at the corner booth?"

"Sounds fine," Kyle answered appreciatively.

As the waitress left, Meg grinned. "I feel like a Hollywood movie star."

"So do I," Kyle replied with a chuckle. "Well, now that we're terribly famous," he said in a fake British accent, "we'll have to be careful and not let it go to our heads."

"Neither one of you is in any immediate danger," Monica interrupted, appearing unexpectedly at their table. "First you have to have heads it can go to." She stood glowering at them.

"Monica!" Kyle smiled broadly. "Our grand-prize winner! I'm delighted to see you."

"Stuff it," she said through clenched teeth. "I saw you when I came in, so I thought I'd drop by your table and warn you."

"About what?" Kyle asked good-naturedly.

"The way I see it, you've declared war. So KLUV is retaliating by launching a promotion that'll annihilate your little station once and for all. We're going to give away an oil well."

"A real one, that works?" Meg asked, aghast.

"You bet," Monica replied snugly. "Also, I'm sure you've heard of that radio soap opera that's been making history with its high ratings? Well, KLUV has acquired syndication rights."

"And when will all this begin?" Kyle asked, his tone taut as he tried unsuccessfully to sound uninterested.

"Tomorrow we'll start advertising our contest, which will begin next week, as will the soap opera."

The minute Monica was out of hearing range, Meg leaned forward. "Kyle, she's really bringing in the heavy artillery."

"Don't worry, I think we can handle it."

"If she takes away a large percentage of our audience, that'll really hurt your advertising revenue."

"Of course it will," Kyle answered.

Spring Madness

"Can the station withstand the financial loss?"

"I think so," he said slowly. "Of course, that all depends on the extent of the damage she inflicts." His mouth tightened. "I think you and I had better start thinking of ways to counter Monica's offensive."

"I'll help all I can," Meg replied. Kyle's features were set in harsh lines. His hands were curled into tight fists. His body communicated his tension despite the casual tone of his words. "Do you think KHAY will survive?" she asked in a whisper.

"We'll just have to wait and see what happens."

She leaned back against the seat cushions. She didn't like the sound of that. She didn't like it at all.

Chapter 8

MEG SAT IN Kyle's office revising the final draft of their American portrait segment. For the past seven days KLUV had been advertising heavily, hoping to gain the maximum audience for what they termed their Extravaganza Week. Today they'd be launching the contest that would net the winner one of Monica's oil wells. It was an outrageously expensive prize, though rumor held that the well was a poor producer. Also, this afternoon would mark the start of the syndicated series "Nightbeat," a radio soap opera about the adventures of an investigative newspaper reporter who worked the graveyard shift.

The news that the popular series would be carried by KLUV had already begun to circulate among the townspeople. To Meg's chagrin, some of KHAY's own employees were talking about tuning in. If only there was some way to counter Monica's scheme to undermine Kyle.

Meg's thoughts were interrupted as Kyle burst into the room. "You won't believe what just happened.

Monica's oil well contest just backfired. Someone already won!"

"Are you serious?" she asked, her voice rising an octive at the unexpected good news. She gestured hastily at his chair. "Sit down and tell me all about it."

He did so, but within seconds he was restlessly pacing the room. His excitement was like a current of electricity that charged the air around them. "I was listening to KLUV while I was driving back to the office, just to see what Monica was up to, and I managed to catch the start of their contest. Their deejay read a list of different subjects, then asked their caller to choose one. He explained to the listeners that a question from a particular category would then be selected at random. Their contestant chose American history, and the deejay asked him to spell the name of President James Madison's wife."

"The only thing that comes to my mind is Dolly Madison, like the ice-cream company," Meg said.

Kyle nodded, laughing. "That's what I thought, too, but there was a trick to it. Well, this man turned out to be a retired university professor, and he not only knew her name, he also knew the right spelling. It's D-O-L-L-E-Y."

"Poor Monica. She was hoping to draw out the contest and the publicity for as long as possible."

Giving a triumphant whoop, Kyle pulled Meg out of her chair and whirled her around exuberantly. "And instead she gets to give away an oil well to the first contestant!" he exclaimed. "All that expense for a one-shot contest!"

Relief and joy flooded through Meg. Swept away by emotion, she wrapped her arms around Kyle in an impulsive hug. "That's great! I can't think of anyone more deserving."

Kyle pulled away far enough to hold her at arm's length. His eyes captured hers. "You don't admire her quite as much anymore, I see."

The realization came as a surprise to Meg. She was

Spring Madness

beginning to feel a great deal of loyalty toward KHAY. "My allegiance is to KHAY, and like it or not, she's this station's mortal enemy."

"You're right about that. There's nothing she'd like more than to buy me out at a rock-bottom price." Kyle returned to his chair and leaned back. "But even with this ratings war she's declared on us, I think our station can hold its own. The latest listings show we're actually up a few percentage points, at KLUV's expense. Do you realize how many invitations are starting to pour in for you and me to do personal appearances? I compiled a list." He pulled a sheet of paper from his pocket. "Smith's Hardware wants us for the dedication of their new lumber counter. The Wildlife Club needs us to swing the first hammer in their Smash a Gas Guzzler fund raiser. There are a bunch more. I want to check with you and see if there's any scheduling conflict as far as you're concerned."

"If there is, there's no reason why you can't go alone and represent KHAY. Those are great opportunities to promote the station, and you shouldn't pass them up."

She hoped he'd agree. Promotional appearances could play a large part in KHAY's battle for survival. Only one thing worried her. Their teasing and innuendo on the show suggested a romantic involvement between Kyle and her. If people expected them to act that way in public, too, then things might get darned awkward. How could she avoid thinking of Kyle in more romantic terms if she was forced into such a role? It was undoubtedly the coward's way out, but she was hoping to avoid the matter altogether.

"As much as I personally dislike being out in front of a crowd, I think we should go together," Kyle said thoughtfully. "These invitations come to Rager and Randall. The listeners want both of us. To them we're not two separate people—we're a team."

"That means we're projecting ourselves as we intended to," she said, hedging. Publicity appearances were usually something she enjoyed doing. But in this case there was an added element that made the situation too risky for her taste.

Kyle glanced down at the papers in front of him. "I'll tell you what. We both agree that these appearances are important. However, since neither of us is really enthused about doing them, let's compromise. It'll be quite a bit of work, but for now let's accept ten invitations per month. The more publicity we can generate to counter Monica's offensive, the better off we'll be."

Reluctantly she agreed.

Although KLUV's contest died before it had a chance to increase the ratings, in the two weeks that followed KHAY began to feel the effects of KLUV's new programming. The number of callers who contacted them during their show began to decrease noticeably.

Though Kyle claimed not to be worried, Meg sensed his consternation. After their Tuesday morning show she gathered her courage and decided to broach the subject.

"Kyle, we're going to have to come up with a way to counter the following Monica's soap opera is acquiring." He stopped typing his script on tips for growing better houseplants and leaned back in his chair to listen. "By running two episodes daily, she's taking our audience away from us. People tune in, then stick with KLUV's programs instead of switching the dial back to KHAY."

"Her budget is practically limitless, Meg," Kyle said. "There isn't anything I can do to compete with an expensive syndicated series like 'Nightbeat.'"

"How about bringing in some other syndicated programs that aren't as costly?" she suggested. "Maybe the top-oldies type of thing."

"I just don't have it in our budget," he said. "I'm stretched to the limit as it is."

"You're still losing money?" she asked hesitantly.

"No," he admitted. "I'm running in the black because of our increased advertising revenue, but I'm turning practically every dime I make back into the station for

Spring Madness

things like new office and broadcasting equipment. The trouble with having purchased an existing station is that most of the equipment is several years old. At this moment I'm trying to set enough aside to make a substantial down payment on a new transmitter. Otherwise I won't be able to meet the payments."

"Well, we won't keep our new sponsors, let alone gain additional ones, if we start losing our audience."

Kyle turned up his palms in a gesture of resignation. "I'll fight like hell to keep that from happening, but if our accounts start to bail out, there's nothing I can do."

"Maybe we're looking at this problem all wrong," Meg said, putting her pen down. She was working at a card table Kyle had recently set up for her inside his office. At least now she didn't have to use the floor as a desk!

"How so?"

For several moments she remained silent, her thoughts racing. "We could do a spoof of 'Nightbeat,' incorporating enough differences into the material to avoid legal problems. Our own story line could loosely parallel the series Monica's airing. If we make ours funny, and run it an hour after her scheduled episodes, I'm sure people will start tuning back to us."

Kyle smiled brightly. "Boy, am I glad you're on my side."

She grinned. "I'm the yin to your yang. See, sometimes you get too bogged down, thinking of what you could buy if you had the money, instead of trying to use the resources you've already got available."

He regarded her with admiration. "I think Aunt Kate's right. We *do* make a perfect team." He took her hands in his, his thumbs brushing her wrists in feather-light caresses.

A sweet weakness spread through her. Her heartbeat began to drum at an erratic tempo as she fought the temptation to step into his arms. Her skin tingled with excitement. "Kyle," she said with impulsive sincerity, "for the first time in months I feel truly happy. We *do* make a great team, and I'm glad it's turned out this way. Working for you, and KHAY," she added quickly, suddenly feeling unaccountably embarrassed, "has been the best thing I've ever done for myself."

His blue eyes shone with an intensity that left her breathless. "Why do you think that is?" he asked softly.

The second she had uttered the words, she sensed the folly of making the earnest admission. "I, uh..."

He grazed her cheek with his palm. "Can't you bring yourself to say it, Meg?"

"You know I like you, Kyle. We're friends. What more is there to say?" She had the distinct impression that her face was turning deep scarlet, but she pretended to focus her attention back on the paperwork in front of her. To admit anything more would be a mistake. "I think I'll start the script right now. I'm going to call our spoof 'Nightly.'"

"There's more to our team than just friendship, you know," he pursued.

Gathering all her courage, she forced herself to meet his eyes. His scent was masculine, his lips inviting, and he was just inches away. For an instant she felt herself drowning in his gaze. With a concerted effort she pulled herself to the shores of reason. "Yes," she said, there's this little matter of work, which we're not getting done."

"You're avoiding the issue," he insisted.

"You noticed," she replied boldly.

The first week was the hardest. Between racing against the clock to write the script, and keeping track of Monica's broadcasts, they barely had time for anything except work.

It was Saturday morning, fifteen minutes before they were to sign off. Meg read the last few lines of their "Nightly" segment: "'Knowing his job was completed, intrepid reporter Harry Newsflash placed his fedora back on his head and walked out of the police station. The librarian's sinister plot had been uncovered, and no one would ever again obliterate the explicit scenes from D.H. Lawrence's *Sons and Lovers* with red crayon.'"

Spring Madness 99

Meg placed cartridges in the machine, and soon taped music was on the air.

Kyle removed his headphones and simultaneously reached for the telephone receiver. The switchboard light seemed to glow incessantly these days. "No, our next installment won't be aired until Monday," he told an enthusiastic fan.

Meg turned the console over to the afternoon deejay, then walked out into the hall. She couldn't remember the last time she had felt so completely exhausted.

Kyle joined her. "I thought this week would never end." He rubbed the back of his neck.

"We've accomplished what we set out to do," she said, "but I'm ready to expire. I've never worked so hard or slept so little in my entire life!"

"I have some news that might make you feel better," he offered.

"What's that?" She glanced at him as they traversed the hall to his office. A lock of pale golden hair had fallen across his forehead, as it often did, making him look infinitely appealing to her. Her eyes drifted downward to the length of virile arm exposed by his rolled-up sleeves. He communicated an aura of power in the way he moved, an unflagging strength that seemed to come from the very core of him. His nearness filled her with restless longing.

"I've hired a copywriter to take some of the pressure off us by writing the household hints and profiles," he said, the deep timbre of his voice sending lightning-hot flames to the very center of her being.

"That's great, but I thought you couldn't afford it," she replied with a casualness she was far from feeling.

He held the door open for her. "I can now. KHAY picked up two new sponsors this week, thanks to your spoof."

"I saw some of the mail that came in," Meg said, dropping into the nearest chair, "and from the sound of it, we've caught on."

"I know how much extra work this has been for you,

Meg." He gave her an apologetic look and enveloped her hand in his large, warm palm. "Particularly since I've been tied up all week trying to keep our transmitter working." He gave her hand a gentle squeeze, but didn't let go.

"I managed." Strength flowed from his touch, revitalizing her. Her blood raced hotly as her thoughts turned to vivid images of what could happen between them if she lowered her guard.

"I just want you to know that I really appreciate all you've done. You're really something."

"The entire staff has been putting in lots of extra time," she replied a bit too rapidly, embarrassed by her inability to control her errant imagination. "Patsy stayed at her desk until ten o'clock one night typing the sales letters you wanted to send to different businesses."

"I can't believe how everyone's pitched in. I guess word got around that KHAY needed a little extra help."

"They did it because of the loyalty they feel toward you. I want you to know that. You may not have the budget to pay top salaries, but they appreciate the fact that you really care about them. I heard Patsy telling one of the deejays that you gave her the week off with pay when her dad got sick. Things like that have really endeared you to them." And to her, she added silently.

"And how do you feel?" he asked quietly.

"I think you're a very special man, Kyle." His masculinity was a magnetic force that wrapped itself around her, weaving an entrancing spell that left her feeling vulnerable and disconnected.

He gently pulled her up out of the chair. Standing inches away, he held her gaze for a brief eternity.

The unspoken communication tore the breath from her lungs. She wanted to run, to force the desire that smoldered within her far into the recesses of her soul, where it couldn't hurt her. Yet something more powerful prevented her from doing either.

"Yet, when all is said and done, you're still not ready to trust me," he stated with unmistakable disappointment.

Spring Madness 101

"Don't you see?" She tried to find the words to express her confused feelings. "I just don't want to be hurt again. If I don't let myself care for you, then I'm safe."

"You'd be safe anyway, Meg, but I guess I'll have to let you discover that for yourself." He moved away from her.

His withdrawal left her feeling empty. Wouldn't she ever be happy? She kept telling herself and Kyle that she didn't want to get involved, but was it already too late? When he drew away, she felt as if her heart had suddenly gone into a deep freeze. "Kyle, I do care," she said.

He turned and smiled. "That's a start, Meg."

The intercom buzzer sounded, interrupting him. After a brief conversation he glanced up. "You know, I just had a great idea."

"What's that?"

"Everyone's really been terrific about working to keep KHAY in competition. Why don't we throw a party here at the station tonight? We'll celebrate the team spirit that kept us going, and the fact that we're back in the running again."

"You're right," she agreed. "That's a great idea."

It took the rest of the day to arrange the details, but by seven that evening every member of the staff had showed up at the station to celebrate. T. J. McKay was working the evening shift that night and several other people were in the booth with him. The musical selections from his show were being piped into every room. Some of the office staff, including Patsy and her date, were dancing in the hall outside the sound booth.

People moved about in small groups, drinking punch and selecting cold cuts and desserts from a heavily laden table, while other people gave their spouses or dates a grand tour of the station. Ted, the midnight disk jockey, waved and raised his cup of coffee in a toast. Meg and Kyle laughed from across the room and returned his salute.

When Ted turned away to speak to another guest,

Kyle, looking magnificent in light gray slacks and a navy sport-jacket, grasped Meg's forearm and gently pulled her into the shadows of an unlit hallway. "You look great in that dress tonight," he murmured.

The ivory Quiana draped smoothly over her body, accentuating her height and slender curves. "I'm glad you're pleased," she replied softly. "By the way, I don't know if you've noticed, but everyone here feels very much a part of this station. I've worked in many different places, Kyle, but I've never experienced this kind of loyalty. It takes one heck of man to generate those feelings."

"And are you glad we're a team, Meg?" He rested his arms lightly on her shoulders, clasping his hands behind her neck.

He stood so close. The temptation to melt into his arms was like an unbearable ache inside her.

Then, as if she'd been struck by a lightning bolt, she realized that she was falling in love with him! The realization left her dazed and more than a little scared. But more than anything, she wanted to tell him how she felt.

She answered his question carefully, with painful honesty. "I wanted to go solo at one time, Kyle. I thought that's what would make me happy. But I was wrong. I wouldn't trade what we have for anything. I'm not sure when it happened, but you and I have become so close it's as if we're a part of each other. I like the way you care about people, and"—she hesitated, then continued boldly—"I like the feelings you bring out in me, even though they scare me half to death. You're more than just a boss and a good friend, Kyle. And that's the most frightening and terrific thing that's happened to me in a long time."

"Oh, Meg." With a groan he pulled her farther into the darkness and guided his mouth to hers. Passion whipped against them, leaving Meg trembling. His need thrilled her, as did the knowledge that it was she who evoked his response.

"Let's sneak away." He gave her a devilish smile,

glancing at the others from their hidden vantage point. "We've already talked with everyone here. They'll never miss us."

She nodded, wanting him more than she had ever dreamed possible. The realization that she cared deeply for him, and the thrill of that admission, left her excited and anxious like never before. Allowing him to draw her to his side and hold her there tightly, she walked with him to the rear exit.

The full moon was their companion as they drove to Kyle's house. Though short, the trip heightened the electric tension that stretched taut between them. Unresolved longing tore at them, straining their patience.

Kyle's hand covered hers. "Meg, there are so many things I've wanted to say to you, but now the words won't come." He pulled into his driveway and brought the car to a stop.

Meg buried her face against his shoulder. "Then don't tell me," she whispered. "Show me what you want me to know."

Without hesitating he scooped her from the passenger's side and carried her across the driveway to the front door. "I want tonight to be even better than any fantasy you've ever had, Meg," he said as he carried her across the threshold. "I want us to undress emotionally so we can see each other as we are, vulnerable yet strong because of the feelings we share."

He carried her into the bedroom and lowered her gently onto his bed. Holding her against his chest, he whispered, "Tonight we'll discover each other, my sweet lady, and I'll do everything in my power to make that journey one you'll never forget."

The rawness in his voice, the softness of his touch, created a stormy maelstrom that left her quaking with desire. He robbed her of her senses. A yearning too powerful to resist crested like a wave that threatened to engulf her, leaving her breathless and weak. The taut, muscular strength in his body compelled the primitive woman in her to surrender.

"Kyle, don't make me wait," she whispered in an agonized plea. "I need and want all the love you can give me."

"The night's young. Be patient," he murmured, soothing her with his caresses.

He nipped at her sensitized skin, teasing and pleasuring her with the skilled ministrations of a man experienced in the art of love. Her desire grew as she sensed the barely leashed hunger in him. With a groan he pulled her to her feet and began to undress her. Garments dropped one by one to the carpeted floor as he bared her to his gaze, his eyes sizzling over her naked flesh. Lips, warm and seeking pressed against her temple, then slowly moved across her cheekbones, coming to rest at the base of her throat.

Meg shivered and buried herself in the tenderness of his embrace. Desperately she sought a release from the unbearable tension that was building inside her. The sweet torment robbed her of all her strength, and she leaned against him for support.

His arms wrapped tightly around her waist as he pushed her backward onto the bed. His hand drifted lazily over the swell of her breasts, molding and shaping the pliant flesh. Bathed in the soft glow of moonlight filtering through the sheer curtains, Meg watched him undress, her gaze lingering on the curling expanse of hair that covered his powerful torso. In the semidarkness he looked powerfully masculine and infinitely arousing.

Instinctively she reached out to touch him, but he remained just out of her grasp. In one fluid motion he unclasped his belt and finished removing his clothes. The lean length of his body, and the sight of his aroused manhood, sent an exhilarating thrill coursing through her.

Her lips parted involuntarily as he bent over her, his body poised. She arched her back as he bent to kiss her taut nipples. She dug her fingers in his thick hair, pressing her face against him. "You make me want you," she murmured in a ragged voice.

"Then let me fill your dreams with only thoughts of me," he whispered savagely.

Meg drowned in a tumult of fiery sensations as Kyle explored the intimate recesses of her body. She invited all he could give, knowing that her surrender would make him burn as she did, with the white-hot flame of passion.

She exulted in the need that drove him to make her yield completely to him, but it was his tenderness that pierced her heart. "Make love to me, Kyle," she pleaded, arching her hips in an age-old invitation.

She gasped at the first shuddering impact, feeling her body become one with his. She cried out his name as he forged deep within her, and a rainbow of sensations flooded her senses. Her fingers clung to the tight muscles of his shoulders as she gave herself completely, holding nothing back, seeking the ultimate union.

As he drove into her one final time, the world came apart, then shuddered in delicious ecstasy...

For long moments neither of them moved. Kyle lifted his head and nuzzled the base of her throat. "Lady, the things you do to me," he whispered.

Meg opened her eyes slowly. "Have I only dreamed you, or are you real?"

His mouth covered hers. "By the time the sun rises, you won't have the slightest doubt."

Chapter 9

SUNLIGHT DANCING ON Meg's pillow nudged her awake. She felt warm beneath the covers. Kyle's arms were still entwined around her as he pressed her against his hard chest, weaving a protective cocoon. Finding comfort in the steady rise and fall of his chest, she rested her forehead against his neck and sighed contentedly. Slowly reality began to seep into her consciousness.

An uneasy feeling spread through her as she remembered the last time she had awakened in a man's arms. Painful memories of her years as Mike's wife came flooding back. The sensual side of her nature had seduced her into an ill-fated marriage. Had she once again allowed physical needs to taint her judgment?

She edged gently away. As she looked down at Kyle's sleeping face, her heart melted and her worries faded away. She bent down and kissed him gently. Prudent or not, she had fallen in love with Kyle Rager, and for the present there was little she could do except enjoy it.

Kyle stirred as she slipped out of bed. "Good morning," he murmured sleepily.

"You're beautiful when you first wake up," she teased. "You look cuddly and rumpled in a pleasant sort of way."

"Come back down here with me," he said, pulling her back onto the pillows. "Instead of trading compliments with you, I'd rather show you how much you mean to me."

She wriggled away. "I'm hardly ever in a romantic mood when I look like Mr. Hyde—and I usually do before eight in the morning."

"You're beautiful," he insisted, "and downright feisty before breakfast."

"Speaking of breakfast," she said, dressing quickly, "I do hope you intend to treat me to a sumptuous meal."

He groaned and tossed the covers back to stand up. Though completely naked, he walked around the room without a trace of self-consciousness. "You win. I'm up. And to show you what a good sport I am, I'll cook you the best pancake breakfast you've ever had."

Twenty minutes later Kyle slid a giant pancake from the griddle onto a plate. "It ran," he mumbled apologetically.

She shrugged. "It looks like a crêpe."

"Don't be picky," he growled, taking the enormous second pancake for himself.

Meg bit into hers and chewed the rubberlike substance with great caution, wondering if she'd dare try to swallow it.

Kyle's eyes locked with hers as he gulped down a mouthful. "This tastes like"—he searched for the right comparison—"old sneakers smell."

"I agree," she said, staring at her plate.

"I'll make a deal with you," he said, tossing his pancake into the garbage can. "If you'll forget all about pancakes, I'll treat you to the best toast and coffee in town."

"You've got it," Meg said, relieved.

Spring Madness   109

As the coffee began to brew, Kyle joined her at the table. "By the way, we acquired a new advertising client yesterday, Kelly's Greenhouse. We're going to have to produce a spot for him. He bought time during our morning show."

"Okay. No problem. We'll just ad-lib something like we normally do. It sounds much more natural that way."

"I hate doing that, Meg. I wish you'd let me stick to a script for things like this. It's more professional."

"When we go with the flow, so to speak," she replied, "it reaches the listeners more effectively than just airing another taped promotion. They're tired of hearing those, and more than likely they'll switch stations and tune in to someone else who's playing music."

"I can see ad-libbing our own show, but advertising is a completely different situation. A script would ensure that we cover all the major points in a minimum amount of time. Otherwise, we end up rambling."

"I don't think so," she countered. "And none of the clients has ever complained."

"I can't tell you how much I hate to feel pressured like that on the air. I'm always concerned that we won't cover the material we're supposed to, or that I'll say something wrong and misrepresent the product."

She gave him a quizzical look. "Is it really that hard for you?"

"It is," he said matter-of-factly. "If you had one ounce of compassion you'd make my life easier by giving in and agreeing to work the spots from a script."

She pursed her lips. "I hate scripts," she muttered.

He covered her hand with his own. "But you're fond of me, and think what you'd be doing for my peace of mind," he cajoled.

"All right," she conceded at length. "We'll do it your way."

When the coffee finished brewing, Kyle brought out two cups. "While I get this ready, will you start the toast?"

"Sure."

"You know, Meg, I'm really glad you agreed to do the commercials my way."

She was buttering a slice of toast when the realization struck her. The one thing she had always considered sacred was her style on the air. She radiated a relaxed aura simply because she worked her way. Now, having lowered her guard around Kyle, she was making concessions that directly affected her performance on the job! Love had entered her life once again, and almost immediately she had started to weaken. How could she have agreed to do something that went against her very nature?

Love! She had no intention of catering to that emotion if it meant that she'd lose the ability to stand up for herself.

And here she was fixing his breakfast! She slammed the butter knife down on the counter. "Listen, I've changed my mind about breakfast. I think it's time for me to go home."

He looked up in dismay. "What brought this on?" he demanded, clearly perplexed. "Did my horrible pancakes offend you?"

"Kyle, look at us." She waved a hand around the kitchen. "This little domestic scene is cute and all that, but it isn't what I want for myself. What happened last night was natural. We both felt a physical attraction, and one thing led to another. But let's not kid ourselves into believing it was more than that."

His eyes bored into her. "Are you listening to yourself? You really should, you know. You're so afraid to love someone that the remotest possibility makes you run back into your shell. I thought our partnership went deeper than just business. Or is success all you're really interested in? If so, you've got a very empty existence to look forward to."

"That's not true, and you know it. I'm just trying to take care of myself. I've had enough hurt in my life, and I certainly don't intend to look for more." Anger seeped through her like an icy chill. "You're just mad because you can't accept the fact that I'm not about to pine away at your feet just because we had sex last night."

It took only a cursory glance at him to realize how much her words had hurt him. She wanted to take them back, but it was too late.

"Fine," he said, his voice taut. "If that's the way you feel, then go ahead and leave."

She made a grand exit, or at least she hoped it would pass as one. But as she walked outside into the cool morning air, she realized with dismay that she had arrived in his car!

Someone up in the heavens must hate her, she decided. Without a taxi or bus, her only alternative was to walk the six miles to the radio station. Despite her desperation, she rejected the idea and returned to Kyle's front door. She knocked softly.

He opened the door and stood boldly on the threshold, fully dressed. "Remember how you got here now, huh?" He sounded irritatingly smug. "Do you want me to drive you back to the station?"

Meg stopped herself from uttering an unkind retort. Maybe if she was nicer, he'd understand that, although she couldn't make love with him anymore, she still hoped they'd remain friends. "It's a long walk to where my car is parked," she managed to say, hoping he'd take the remark as a *yes*.

"If you'd like a ride, all you have to do is ask for one." He leaned against the doorframe and studied her speculatively.

More than anything else at that moment she wanted to kick him soundly in the shins. "Would you please give me a ride back to my car?" she asked. It took all her willpower, but she uttered the entire sentence without raising her voice.

"Certainly. It would be my pleasure," he replied with exaggerated politeness.

Meg followed Kyle to his car in unnerving silence. Several minutes into the trip she said, "You're not talking."

"Neither are you."

"This is childish. We're still business associates."

"If you don't care about me—not really, as you pointed out before—why are you making such a big deal out of this?" he countered arrogantly.

She contemplated walking the rest of the way after all. They were almost halfway to the station, and the thought of hiking three miles suddenly seemed a great deal more attractive than staying in the car with him. "Kyle, do you want to make me crazy?" she demanded. "Because if that's your goal, you're doing a wonderful job."

He simply smiled.

She leaned back in her seat and decided to ignore him. If only she had brought her car! Why couldn't life be a little more cooperative this morning?

Several minutes later he dropped her off at the station's parking lot. "See you at work," he said with a hint of warning in his tone.

Did he mean the comment as a threat? She stared at him for a moment, then turned away. Probably not. In fact, if there was any justice in this world, he was probably as confused as she was at the moment.

Feeling a great deal of empathy for the Amazons who never allowed men on their land, she slammed the door of his car and strode over to her own.

On Monday morning, feeling in a slightly better mood, Meg walked into Kyle's office, determined never to allow their relationship to become as intimate and personal again. She just wasn't ready to relinquish control of her life to another man, especially not to her boss.

"We've got one hour before air time," she told him. "I have to finish the final draft of our spoof of 'Nightbeat.' Did you remember to tape KLUV's episode today so we'll know what's going on?"

"Don't worry about writing the script. I've already done it. I had to come in early this morning to do some maintenance work on the transmitter, and since I had some time on my hands after I finished, I went ahead and took care of it."

"Great." She began to work on the program log. "Anything special you want on the air today?"

"Why not try something a little different? We'll go ahead and play our soap, then let the show take whatever direction seems best at the time."

She looked up in surprise. That didn't sound like the Kyle she knew. "Say that again?"

"You heard me."

"This isn't like you." She gave him a wary look. "What's going on?"

"All along you've been telling me I'm too inflexible. I've decided you might have a point. You're more experienced than I am as a disk jockey, so maybe I'm the one who should learn from your methods. It might even help the ratings. But now, instead of being pleased that I'm trying to adopt your carefree style, you act as if you feel threatened."

"I do not feel threatened," she protested.

"Good," he replied, interrupting her before she could say anything else.

This was not going to be a good day, Meg decided. She stared at the newspaper before her, scanning the headlines for bits of information to use as commentary during their program. But all she could think about was the conviction that Kyle was definitely planning something.

She tried to ignore her suspicions, but curiosity proved to be too much for her. By the time they began their morning broadcast, she felt as if she were sitting on pins and needles.

The first half hour proceeded smoothly. Then came time to read the segment of "Nightly" that Kyle had written. Their intrepid hero, Harry Newsflash, had found love. But the object of his affections had locked herself in a closet, claiming that every time she fell in love she lost control of her appetite and gained ten pounds.

As Kyle read the script, Meg felt the blood drain from her face.

> So, Melinda, afraid to face the possibility of love, left Harry's arms and ran for the closet. "Love and I are mortal enemies," she wailed. "Leave me. Save yourself for someone who blossoms in beauty, not girth."
>
> "Melinda, my sweet, come out. Let me take care of you. You need never fear my love."
>
> "I'll never come out," she vowed. "I'm going to hide away in my nice safe closet for the rest of my life."
>
> "But, Melinda, don't you see? If you stay in there, you'll languish away all alone. Love carries risks, but it also promises life."
>
> Slowly the closet door opened. Melinda peered out, then jumped into Harry's arms. "You're right. I don't want to go on without you. I'll risk the weight gain. You're worth it!" she declared happily.
>
> "And I'll help you lose those pounds again. Married people have their ways, you know."

As Kyle concluded, he gave Meg a flirtatious wink.

Meg's face burned. "Are you crazy?" she whispered furiously.

"Now I have a question for you folks out there," Kyle told the audience. "If a man is in love with a woman who's afraid to admit her feelings, what's the best way to help her get over that fear?"

Calls began to come in.

"He should love her and be patient, don't you think, Meg?" a woman caller asked.

Meg choked. "I...uh..."

Kyle grinned. "What do you think, Meg? Answer the lady."

She fought the sudden, inexplicable urge to run out

of the booth and let out a primal scream. "Well," she said, searching desperately for an answer, "maybe in certain cases the man should give up."

The light announcing another caller began to blink on and off.

"What I'd do is treat the lady with all the tenderness I had and eventually she'd come around," a young man drawled. "Women are like colts, you know. You can spook them if you move too fast."

"There's sage wisdom, Kyle," Meg teased. "Maybe you should take notes."

"I'm curious," the next caller ventured. "Kyle, ol' buddy you wouldn't be alluding to a romance between you and Meg, would you?"

Meg slithered down in her chair and covered her face with her hands.

"Our Meg, afraid of anything? Naw!" Kyle told their listener.

Sensing a way to change the conversation to a topic she'd feel more comfortable with, Meg said, "Fear's an interesting thing to speculate on. For instance, what frightens men?"

"We'll let our audience think about that while we play the next selections," Kyle intoned.

As soon as the microphones were turned off, Meg glared at him. "Are you out of your mind? I've never been so embarrassed in all my life."

"Really? And to think I can evoke all that emotion in you," he quipped.

"You're sadistic!"

"But you love me anyway."

"I don't love anyone!" she protested defiantly. "And you might as well accept that fact."

"Sorry. That's one thing I can't accept."

As their taped selections reached an end, Kyle switched the microphones back on.

"I know what men are afraid of," a woman caller ventured. "They're terrified of not being good in sports. To them, being athletic means that they're real men. Ever notice how they'll cheerfully kill themselves just to win a game of basketball or tennis?"

Meg chuckled. "I think women everywhere would agree with that."

"Hey, that's not fair," Kyle interjected. "Athletic women are the same way. In fact, I think women compete harder than men."

"I wouldn't know." Meg sighed. "I'm not very much into sports. In fact, my idea of hell was taking gym class."

"Then you're intimidated by sports?" Kyle asked tauntingly.

"Not on your life. I'm not an athlete, but I could hold my own with most other adults who chose sports as a way to punish their bodies."

"If you had to choose a sport—one you think you could be reasonably competent in—which would you choose?" Kyle asked Meg, then their listeners.

"I'd choose softball," Meg replied. "It looks like the simplest. Basketball is my second choice, but the thought of fighting a solid wall of people just so I can dump the ball into something that looks like a defective aerial wastebasket leaves me bored."

"Did you know that KLUV is sponsoring a physical fitness month?" one caller informed them. "You guys sound as if you could use the exercise. Sitting around all day isn't good for the body."

Kyle laughed. "What do you mean? Even in our current physical condition we could outdo KLUV at almost anything. In fact, since we've been discussing sports..." Pushing the button for a clear line, he began to dial the disk jockey at KLUV.

Meg stared at him, aghast.

"This is Kyle Rager from KHAY, Jon, and we're on the air right now. The reason I'm calling is that I hear you people have a physical fitness project going. Since we want to prove to everyone that KHAY's jocks are far superior in every way—with or without a defined physical fitness regimen—we'd like to challenge your station to a softball game."

The disk jockey hedged. "I'd have to check this out first, Kyle."

"Well, of course, if KLUV doesn't feel it can compete..."

"We'd be glad to compete, Rager," Jon replied somewhat hesitantly, "but we'd have to work out the details."

"I'll tell you what. Talk to your people, and then get back to us. The proceeds from the game will benefit a charity we mutually agree on."

It took twenty minutes for KLUV to come back with an official response. "We need some time to make the arrangements," Monica Hanrahan said over the speakers, "but how about the last Saturday of this month, at J. Edgar Hoover High's baseball field?"

"You've got it," Kyle promised.

"We'll have all our jocks and some of our staff there, since we're going to need at least nine people on the field."

"It's all set, then."

"I'll be looking forward to it. Oh, and Kyle," she added sweetly, "all the jocks have to play—whether or not they know diddly squat about softball."

Meg shook her head vigorously. "Wait a minute."

Kyle held up his hand. "No problem at all."

As soon as the music began, Meg turned angrily to him. "I can't believe you've done this to me! First you turn a private feud into a public competition; then you drag me into it. Kyle, I've never been able to hit a ball in my life! In high school I was always the last one chosen for the teams. Even when we played basketball, despite my size I was never coordinated enough to be of any use on the court."

"I'll teach you. Don't worry."

"Of course I'll worry," she retorted flatly as she turned her attention back to the console. "It's one of my specialties."

Chapter 10

MEG SAT IN Kyle's office, taking sips from a can of cola. "The response we've received to our proposed softball game during these past two days has been great," she said. "People seem really enthusiastic. They know KLUV and KHAY have been embroiled in some pretty tough competition, and now they can't wait to see it made public."

"It'll be fun, too, though I'm sure there are some people"—Kyle grinned—"who don't agree with me."

"I still don't see why you let Monica insist that *all* the jocks be included," Meg complained.

"You'll be all right; we'll cover for you, I promise. If you're playing in left field, we'll make sure the center fielder or first baseman backs you up on fly balls or grounders. And you can relay the ball to the second baseman when you throw in to the infield. As for the rest, when I gave you some batting practice yesterday, you did okay. You hit nearly every ball I pitched to you."

She groaned. "Yes, and they all traveled a very impressive two feet."

"Hey, Monica's team will have to work to get to them quickly, and by that time you'll already have arrived at first base." He shuffled through a stack of papers on his desk. "By the way, what do you think of having everyone from our station get together at Aunt Kate's after the game? We'll throw a celebration party."

"And what if we lose?" Meg challenged.

"We can't lose, sweetheart. Not with all the publicity we're getting. Don't you see? It's not the softball game itself that matters, but the fact that we're getting people better acquainted with KHAY."

"But for every shred of advertising KHAY gets, KLUV is getting equal time."

"Yes, like it or not, KLUV's ratings have consistently been higher than ours," he admitted. "But since their listening audience is larger, the more often they mention KHAY on their airwaves, the more people we'll reach." He grinned smugly.

"I see your point."

"And whether we win or lose, the town will benefit. Our donation will help buy television sets for the children's ward at Valley Hospital." As he opened the top drawer of his desk in search of a pen, he added, "So, what do you think? Should KHAY have a party?"

Meg nodded. "From the standpoint of morale, I think it's an excellent idea. If we lose, it'll be good to remind everyone that we've still gained a great deal. Of course, if we win, we'll have one heck of a celebration."

"Then the matter's settled. I'll call Aunt Kate. She's been asking me for a long time to bring everyone over. She loves fussing around, baking, and getting her home ready for guests."

"Wait." Meg grimaced. "I completely forgot to tell you. Kate asked me to deliver a message to you this morning. Her sister called last night, and they spoke on the telephone for hours. Kate really misses her, and since Anne can't come down, Kate's decided to leave for California late today for a visit. She'll be gone for at least ten days."

Kyle groaned. "And I bet she's just about cleared out her savings account to get enough money to go."

"I wouldn't know about that."

"Oh, there's no doubt in my mind." His eyes met hers in a plea. "I need your help. I want to go to Aunt Kate's house right now, before she leaves, and convince her to let me pay her expenses. She really doesn't have money for plane fare, and if I know her, she's probably arranged to take the bus."

"Now that you mention it, I think she did say something about driving time."

Kyle swore softly. "I knew it. Look, come out with me. I've got to talk her out of this. She'd be much more comfortable on a plane, and I wouldn't worry so much about her."

"One thing I've learned about Kate is that she's got a mind of her own," Meg warned. "Neither one of us is going to dissuade her, if she's already made up her mind."

"I'd still like to try."

"All right. I'll be glad to help you any way I can."

"Thanks."

Meg followed Kyle in her car. One of the major differences between Kyle and Mike, she concluded, was that Kyle really cared about people. Mike had cared only when it suited his needs. As she pulled into traffic, she kept her eyes glued on the vehicle ahead of her. Maybe it wouldn't be so bad to love and be loved by a man like Kyle.

She shook her head suddenly. What in the world was the matter with her? That kind of thinking was bound to get her into trouble. She smirked. As if she didn't have her hands full with Kyle already!

When they arrived at Kate's house, the older woman was pulling two medium-sized suitcases onto the porch. "Hi!" She waved to both of them.

"Aunt Kate, what are you doing?" Kyle demanded, sounding appalled.

"Didn't Meg tell you? I'm going to visit Anne in California. The bus leaves in forty-five minutes."

Kyle closed his eyes in exasperation. "Aunt Kate, be reasonable! You can't take a bus all the way out there! That'll take over a day. It would be rough on someone *our* age, let alone yours."

"Oh, fiddlesticks! I can handle it perfectly well." She smiled affectionately. "But thank you for your concern anyway."

Kyle turned silently to Meg for help. "Kate," she said, "it's not that he doesn't want you to go. He'd just feel better if you'd take a plane. You'd be there in just a few hours."

"Heavens! I could never afford that."

"But, Aunt Kate, I'll be glad to pay for it," Kyle insisted.

"Didn't you just tell me the other day that in two months you'd have enough cash to put a down payment on a new transmitter?"

"Yes, but..."

She held up a hand. "This would set you back needlessly." She opened the door and walked back inside the house. "Now, come in and we'll have some lemonade before my taxi gets here."

"Taxi? I could have taken you to the station!" Kyle said dejectedly.

Kate led the way to the kitchen and poured three tall glasses of lemonade. "Kyle, I like being independent. You're my nephew, and if I was ever truly in need, I'd come to you for help. But I also enjoy taking care of myself. I wish you understood that."

"I just hate for you to have to do things the hard way. I'm not rich, but I could help to make life a great deal easier for you."

"But that's not what I want," she said softly. "I need to stand on my own two feet—if for no other reason than to prove to myself that I can."

Meg understood both points of view. Kyle's concern touched her deeply, yet she sympathized with Kate's argument, having used it herself many times with Mike, though admittedly under different circumstances. "Kyle, come outside with me," Meg said abruptly. "I'd liked to talk to you."

Kate gave her an appreciative look, then got busy wiping the kitchen counter.

Meg took Kyle's hand and stepped outside. Late afternoon sunlight bathed the porch.

"Kyle." She stood in front of him, her hand still clasped warmly in his. "I know you care a great deal for Kate, but by doing too much for her, you could rob her of her self-respect. That's important to her. What she's trying to make you understand is that, without self-respect, she really would feel like an old woman. She doesn't want to think of herself as a burden to anyone. It's her independence that keeps her young and vital."

Kyle walked to the front steps and gazed at the vast desert mesa. "I know that what you're saying is true, but to me, loving someone implies doing everything you can to see to their welfare. I'm close to getting my down payment on the transmitter, but so what? If I had to, I'd get by with the one we have for another year."

"But don't you understand? Because Kate loves you, that's the last thing she'd want." Meg paused. Then she added softly, "She has the right to show her love for you, too."

"Good point," he conceded, turning to face her. "Thanks, Meg. I'm glad you're here. You're a good ally, as well as a good friend."

A warm sense of belonging swept over her. Then, just as suddenly, panic set in. She was not a part of Kyle's family. They shared the present—nothing more. It was dangerous to delude herself by pretending otherwise. "You can always count on my friendship, Kyle," she said finally.

He started to speak, then changed his mind. Wordlessly he walked back into the kitchen. "Okay, Aunt Kate. Tell me how I can help you get ready."

"Everything's done, except I didn't get a chance to

bring down the summer quilts from the attic. I want to replace the heavier winter bedcovers. They're in the large trunk. Would you be a love and get them down for me sometime before I return? Just leave them in the laundry room."

"We'll take care of it," Kyle replied with a smile.

The blast of a car horn interrupted them. "There's my cab," Kate said quickly. "I'd better get going." She gave them both quick good-bye kisses. "Take care of each other for me."

Meg glanced at Kyle and nodded. "No problem."

"Have fun."

"I will," Kate said with a wave of her hand. Kyle started to follow her to the door, but Kate stopped him. "I'll get the driver to put my suitcases in the trunk. Just stay here and finish your lemonade, dear."

Meg was touched by the look of concern on Kyle's face. It was evident that although he had gone along with his aunt's request, he didn't feel completely comfortable with it. Maybe that was what love was all about, she mused. Letting people be themselves. She studied Kyle. She could learn so much from him.

He returned to the table and sipped his drink. "If I don't go to the attic and get those quilts down today, I'm going to forget all about it." He set his empty glass in the sink. "Would you like to go up there with me? It's an interesting place. I used to sneak upstairs when I was a kid and play there for hours. There's lots of old stuff in trunks, and, of course, the view of the mesa is spectacular. I remember sitting in the window years ago dreaming about the things I'd do with my life when I grew up."

"Like what, for instance?" Meg prodded gently, following him into the hall.

"Like every other kid, I wanted to be a fireman or a policeman. My other favorite fantasy was owning a cattle ranch and being a cowboy."

Meg smiled. "That's a far cry from the businessman you are today."

"As you get older, reality and logic start replacing daydreams," he said with a bit of sadness. "Making a living at something you're good at begins to take precedence over the excitement of being in a shoot-out with a bank robber."

As they reached the top of the stairs, Kyle switched on a light. "Aunt Kate cleans everything, so I don't think it'll be dusty in there." He inserted a key in the door. "Here we go."

He pushed the door open and stepped cautiously inside. "It's just like I thought—a little musty from being closed up, but perfectly clean." He glanced around and spotted a trunk. "I bet the quilts are inside that."

Meg pointed to the other end of the room. "There's another trunk over there by the window, too."

Kyle strode across the room. "Well, this one's closest, so I'll try it first." As he opened the lid, his face seemed to light up. "I don't believe it! Look at this."

Meg squatted on the floor beside him. "Toys."

"Not just toys. These belong to my brother and me."

Amused, she noted his use of the present tense.

Kyle picked up a child's cowboy hat and placed it on his head. "I used to love this hat. Dad used to have to cajole me into taking it off at night when I went to bed."

Meg picked up a bunch of old comic books. "And to whom does this obviously superb literature belong?"

"Those are valuable. That's Andrew the Annihilator, one of the defenders of truth, justice, and the American way."

"I stand corrected," she replied in mock humility.

Kyle extracted a large photo album. "This is my scrapbook." He began leafing through it. When Mom and Dad moved away, they had Aunt Kate store some things for them, but I had no idea that all this stuff was here!"

Meg rubbed her nose. The attic was clean, but the air was stale. "So you've found your own time capsule, it seems," she said as she rose to open a window.

"I just can't believe this." He set the scrapbook down and began rummaging through the trunk again. "Boy, does this bring back memories." He picked up a water pistol. "My brother and I would declare war on each other, and depending on how charitable we were feeling at the time, we'd fill these with anything from water to ink."

"Your mother must have loved you," Meg commented with a chuckle." She unlocked the window and pulled it up as far as it would go. Fresh air wafted inside.

"Turn on the attic light, will you?" Kyle asked. "It's getting dark in here now that the sun is setting."

As she reached for the cord dangling from the bulb in the center of the ceiling, a gust of wind swept inside and slammed the door shut with a loud bang.

Startled, Meg jumped, snapping the cord she had been holding in her hands. Instantly they were encased in darkness.

Kyle swore softly. "I forgot one detail about this attic. If you don't prop the door open when you open the window, the slightest wind slams it shut. Unfortunately it usually trips the locking mechanism. To get out, you either need someone outside with a key, or you have to take the hinges off. But just in case somebody fixed it, I'll give it a try anyway."

Meg blinked as her eyes adjusted to the lack of light. "I have some bad news," she said.

"Tell me *after* you switch on the light."

"That's the bad news." She exhaled deeply. "I was just pulling the cord when the door slammed. It scared me, and I yanked the cord right off. You're taller. Can you reach up and see if there's enough string left to pull?"

She heard the sounds of movement, then a loud thump and a soft oath.

"What was that?" she whispered.

Kyle grumbled in the darkness. "I guess I forgot about the trunks."

After a bit of shuffling around, Meg thought she heard Kyle pass near her. Suddenly she felt something on her shoulder. Terrified at the thought of spiders she whispered, "Kyle, there's something on me."

"Relax. It's only me," he said just behind her. "I've been feeling my way to the light, but you're the most pleasant thing I've touched so far. Can I keep exploring?" he asked in a teasing tone.

"Watch it, buster, or I'll kick you right in the dark," she threatened playfully. "Just find the light switch."

She sensed Kyle moving toward the center of the room where the bulb was. "The cord's broken off inside the fixture, so that settles that. I'll try the door now. My eyes are more used to the darkness, and I can see a little better, thanks to the light coming under the door from the hallway."

She heard him trying to pull the door open. "Damn, it's locked tight." He fell silent for a few seconds. "No light, no key, no one outside." He exhaled softly. "I think we're in trouble."

"Once the moon comes out, maybe we'll be able to get a better look," Meg said hopefully.

"That's a possibility." Kyle cleared his throat. "Meg, this is my fault. I really apologize for getting you into this fix."

Meg lowered herself carefully to the floor. "How is it your fault? I'm the one who opened the window, then broke the cord on the light switch."

"I should have told you about the draft. I got so involved reminiscing that I didn't pay attention to what you were doing."

They both sat silently for a few minutes.

"My eyes have adjusted a bit," Meg said, "but it's still too dark to see anything but vague shadows."

"I know. You're not afraid of the dark, are you?"

She laughed. "No. Like the old joke says, I'm more afraid of what's *in* the dark."

"In this case, it's only me." He paused. "Then, again, maybe that's been the problem all along."

Meg leaned back against something solid. "It's not you, Kyle. It's me. I know that."

"I just don't understand why you're so afraid to love," he said wearily. "Love isn't something to be afraid of."

"Maybe not for you, but in my experience it is."

"Help me to understand you, Meg, please."

In the darkness it was easier to talk. Wrapping her arms around her raised knees, she said, "Loving someone makes me too weak. It was my eagerness to please Mike that always got me into trouble. He'd take me in his arms, and I'd be lost. He'd make me feel safe and loved, and in return I'd do just about anything he asked. The more I gave, the more he took. I can't change the way I am. If I love someone, I want to give that person everything. I'm not much for halfway measures. But I will never allow a man to use me that way again. I might have pleased Mike for many years, but at the expense of myself—and that's too high a price to pay."

"Not every man loves in the same way Mike did."

"Oh, come on, Kyle. Are you telling me that if you and I were"—she couldn't bring herself to say the words *in love*—"having a relationship, you wouldn't start making demands on me?"

"Of course I would, and you'd make them on me, too. But real love isn't selfish, Meg. I would never ask you to become what I want at the expense of being who you are. It's like you told me downstairs when I wanted to pay for Aunt Kate's ticket. Real love bestows the most precious gift of all—the freedom to be yourself."

Meg swallowed, remembering her own words and the way he had responded to them. Mike and Kyle were not the same. So why couldn't she put the past behind her?

She heard him moving about. "What are you doing?"

"I'm working my way to the other trunk." He paused, then added. "At least I hope I am, because I still can't see clearly enough to identify everything in my path."

"What do you need?"

"I noticed it was getting chilly, so I'm going to grab one of the quilts for you to wrap around yourself. I'll close the window, too."

She heard a dull *thunk* as he ran into an obstacle and swore. "Kyle, please, just stay where you are until the moon comes out. I don't want you to hurt yourself."

Spring Madness 129

"The least I can do is close the window. I can find that easily enough by tracking the source of the breeze." Within a few minutes he worked his way back toward her. Gently he placed his coat around her shoulders. "Here. At least you can wear this."

"But, Kyle, that leaves you in shirtsleeves. Keep it on. At least I've got a long-sleeved velour top."

"No, I'm fine."

She felt guilty. "I'll tell you what. We'll compromise. You keep your coat on, put your arms over me, and we'll cuddle. Your body heat will keep me warm enough."

"Great idea," he said enthusiastically. Kyle slipped his jacket back on, then held one side open so that she could nestle against him. "As soon as we get some light, I promise I'll try to get the door hinges off. I'll do everything I can to make sure you don't have to spend the night in the attic."

He squeezed her gently against his side and brushed his lips against her hair and temple in a gesture of reassurance.

The feather-light pressure of his caresses turned her blood to flame. Her skin quivered beneath his touch.

"At least we're not trapped in one of those cobweb-filled, dungeonlike rooms you see in horror movies all the time," he teased, the hushed timbre of his voice rich with protectiveness. "The only thing we have to worry about is rats."

"What?" she exclaimed, every muscle in her body tensing.

He laughed. "Only kidding. They wouldn't have the gall to show up in Aunt Kate's house."

With a sigh she settled back against him. Slivers of moonlight began to filter into the room, dappling it with soft gray shadows.

"This room was made for daydreams," Kyle said pensively. "Yet all the dreams woven here appear destined to remain out of my grasp."

What could she possibly say? That she needed more time? She wasn't even sure that more time would provide the assurance she sought. Yet the thought of losing him made her heart constrict. What had she gotten herself into? She couldn't win either way. Or could she? Kyle and Mike were as different as north from south. The hope that she and Kyle could make the love work still glimmered in the back of her mind.

She stood and walked to the window. A full moon shone outside. It was a night made for love. She turned back to Kyle. His eyes shone in the pale light, compelling her to give in to the emotions she had tried so hard to keep in check.

He walked toward her. "I think we'd better open this window just a little bit. It's getting a little stuffy in here."

Meg's heart was pounding as he brushed past her and lifted the window slightly, but she stood her ground. When he turned, they were only inches apart. She slipped her arms around his waist and held him tightly.

He looked into her eyes, his own glittering brightly in the reflected light. "If I didn't know better, I'd say you want me to kiss you."

"I . . ." The words became lodged in her throat, but she struggled to speak. "You're special to me, Kyle. I don't know what lies ahead for us, but I want you to know that I really care for you."

"I've known it for a long time."

"You couldn't have," she said, without thinking, "or you would have tried to use it to your advantage."

He regarded her speculatively. "Do you really think so badly of me? Search your heart for the answer, Meg. I think you know me better than that by now."

She felt caught in a vortex of crazy emotions. Nothing seemed to make sense anymore. But in the dim, shifting light one thought blinded all others. Whether or not she said the actual words, she wanted to love him and be loved back tonight.

She wrapped her arms around his neck and pressed herself to him. "You were supposed to think this was your idea."

He needed no other encouragement. Cupping the back

of her neck, he lowered his mouth to hers. "And so it is, sweetheart."

He kissed her, teasing her until her lips were as soft and hungry as he wanted them to be. He entwined his hands in her hair, drawing it away from her face as his tongue plundered the depths of her, seeking to master her senses as well as her heart.

His mouth remained on hers as he ran his hands over her body. Meg felt reality fade, and nothing save the electric sensations coursing through her seemed to matter.

"I want you to be mine completely tonight, Meg. I don't want you to be afraid, or to think of anyone or anything except me."

His words touched her very heart. "You're asking for what you already have," she said simply.

He stepped away from her and took two homemade patchwork quilts from the trunk. He laid one on the floor, then unfolded the other over it to serve as a blanket.

His eyes met Meg's as he walked back toward her. "It's not elegant, but tonight all we need is each other."

The raw timbre of his voice spoke of dark, driving passions, and a tenderness born of love. She followed him back to the quilts and began to undress.

"No," he murmured. "Let me."

She became entranced as a sweet weakness invaded her. His fingers brushed against her hot flesh, searing her skin as he divested her of her garments. Her blouse slipped to the floor, and her skirt followed. With each revelation came a new torment. Kyle's lips sampled every inch of her flesh, tasting, probing, and branding her with the fire of his love. "You're breathtaking by moonlight," he whispered.

She melted into his arms, his chest firm against her cheek "I want to make love to you. I want it to be a night that we'll never forget."

"It already is."

His hand stroked her breast as his lips captured hers once more. Blood roared in her ears. With infinite gentleness he lowered her to the soft quilts.

Standing before her, he undressed, revealing the perfect virile build she had known so intimately once before. Each hard plane and hair-darkened contour seemed edged in flame.

Desire became a force too potent to subjugate. "Come to me," she pleaded softly. "I want to feel you with me now."

As he lowered himself beside her and their bodies touched, their need bridged the gap that words could not fill. Meg reveled in the spiraling feverish want that spread through her, burning hottest at the apex of her thighs. She writhed beneath his touch, loving it, seeking it, inviting all the pleasure only he could bring.

Kyle entered her, the contact controlled yet abandoned in a primitive impulse that demanded all their souls could give.

As the burning flame grew ever brighter, like the legendary phoenix that rose from the ashes, Meg's love carried her beyond the needs of the flesh to a dimension where their spirits burned together and became one. Love, heedless of words, exalted them as it propelled them into a universe of shattering peace.

Chapter 11

MEG AWOKE SHORTLY after dawn. Opening her eyes, she searched the attic for Kyle and found him working on the door.

He turned and smiled. "Good morning. I was going to surprise you by having this opened by the time you woke up, but it looks like it might take a while."

She sat up slowly. "Oh, brother. My back is killing me. The floor was harder than I thought," she joked halfheartedly.

"I promise I'll have you out of here in another thirty minutes, Meg. It's just that with only a pocket knife and some tiny screwdrivers I found in one of the trunks, it's not as easy as I'd hoped."

"Don't worry. Neither of us has to work today, so it won't matter."

"Can you give me a hand? Once I get all the screws out of this top hinge, I'll need you to support the door while I work on the bottom hinge." He chuckled. "I still remember the time my uncle went through the same process. He got locked up here once and decided that very day that he'd buy the type of hinges that you can remove with nothing more than a pocketknife. Unfortunately for us, I guess he never quite got around to it."

As Kyle loosened the last of the three screws at the top, he added, "Okay. All you have to do now is support the door."

Meg leaned against it, but it scarcely felt necessary since nothing seemed to move.

"I'm almost finished," he said, after a few minutes. "Once I am, we'll lift the door aside and prop it against the wall. Then, sometime before we leave, we'll have to put it back up. I don't think Aunt Kate would appreciate coming back to a doorless attic."

Meg laughed. "No, she probably wouldn't." Her eyes strayed over the sinewy musculature of his back, which she had caressed so feverishly the night before. Would their present relationship be enough for him? She recalled his words about their being more than business partners.

"Meg," he said slowly, "I know what you're thinking."

Her eyes widened. "You do?"

"You're worried that after what happened last night I'm going to try and trap you into accepting my demands." He gaved her a level look. "I'm not."

"I wasn't concerned about that at all." She met his eyes, then grinned sheepishly. "I'm a rotten liar, aren't I?"

"I'm glad you saved me the trouble of telling you so."

She sighed. "Let's take it slowly, okay? I'm going to need some time to adjust to what's happened between us, to the change in our relationship. Please be patient with me, and whatever you do, don't pressure me. That'll destroy any chances we might have together."

He nodded in agreement. After working for another two minutes in silence, he cried triumphantly. "That's it! Now step aside and let me get the door." With Kyle taking most of the weight, they slid the loosened door over against the inside wall.

Kyle led the way to the stairs, keeping his arm around Meg's waist as they walked down. "I'll make coffee. Then we can get this door back up."

"Let's make it a quick cup, though. I've got errands to run and a lot of things I want to do today."

Kyle scowled and tensed at her side. "You're doing it to me again, aren't you?"

"What do you mean?"

"You keep running away. We made love last night; now you don't want to stay around me any longer than is absolutely necessary. Why can't you just enjoy my company and let me enjoy yours?" He stopped in midstride and, placing his hands on her shoulders, turned her to face him. "Can't you learn to treat me as a friend?"

She nodded slowly. "You're right."

"Good," he said good-naturedly. "Let's go have that coffee."

In the kitchen Kyle brewed a fresh pot and poured two cups of the steaming liquid.

"At least this should renew our energy before we try to tackle that door again," Meg said.

"We're going to have to work as a team on this. That door weighs about sixty pounds, and it's going to take both of us to hold it in place while I fasten the screws. It's not the weight that's a problem," he explained. "It's the awkwardness of holding it."

"Never fear, Super Handywoman's here," she said brightly.

"I'm not kidding," he warned. "One of us could get hurt."

"I understand," she replied seriously, placing her cup in the sink. "If it's going to be a hassle, we might as well get the job out of the way as soon as possible. I'd hate to have it hanging over me."

Together they returned to the attic. They were in the middle of reattaching the door when the telephone began to ring downstairs.

"I don't believe it," Kyle muttered.

"It must be important. Whoever it is isn't hanging up."

"I'll hold the door. You go answer it," he said reluctantly.

Meg dashed down the stairs. When she returned several minutes later, she noted that he had managed to get the door back on its hinges all by himself.

"It's about time," he mumbled. "What took you so long?"

"It was your accountant. He wants you to meet him at the station so he can go over the accounting books with you."

Kyle groaned. "I was afraid that might happen. I've been so busy with other things, I haven't had time to update the books. Now that I'm finally starting to show a profit, my estimated taxes will be going up, and I'll have to make additional payments."

"Can I help?"

"Not really. I just need to get some figures together for my accountant." He gave the door one final check. "Actually, I should be grateful that the station is no longer a de facto nonprofit organization. If you make money, you pay taxes. Until now we were operating at a loss."

"The price of success, boss." She glanced around the attic. "Listen, I can straighten up the mess here by myself now that the door is back where it should be. Why don't you go ahead?"

He glanced at his watch and nodded. "I tell you what. I'll give you a call as soon as I'm finished at the station. With any luck we might even be able to have dinner together."

"I'll be here. I'm going to relax today, maybe watch some television tonight."

"I wish I could spend the day with you," he said regretfully.

"There will be other days," Meg promised, walking downstairs with him, then giving him a quick good-bye kiss. "Good luck."

* * *

Spring Madness 137

Meg's day went by slowly. When it came to her feelings for Kyle, nothing seemed clear. There were times when she thought she should give in to them and trust him, and others when she felt like running away and never looking back.

Shortly after dinner she switched on the television set and lay down on the couch.

The next sound she heard was the telephone ringing. She woke up with a start. It was eight o'clock. Sometime during the past two hours she must have drifted off to sleep. Rousing herself, she reached for the receiver.

"Hello?"

"It's Kyle. I need your help."

The urgency in his tone made her sit up quickly. "What's the matter?"

"I'm still at the station. I was just getting ready to leave when I got a phone call from Ted McCormick, our nighttime deejay, and Alex Norton, the newsman. They went on a fishing trip together yesterday and were due back this afternoon, but their car broke down, and they're stuck in the middle of nowhere. They called to let me know they'd be at least four hours late."

"Do you want me to fill in for Ted?"

"If you would," he said gratefully. "I'll work the news and get the material from the teletype rewritten to suit our audience while you solo the broadcast."

Meg remembered how hard she had fought for the chance to broadcast by herself. Now the thought of going on the air without Kyle had no appeal. Things certainly had changed. "I'll be there in twenty minutes," she promised.

"Meg, you're terrific. Thanks."

When she arrived at the station she immediately relieved the last deejay, who had already worked two hours past his usual shift. The transition went smoothly. Without hesitation Meg took charge of the booth and began to play the logged program selections.

But as it approached eleven o'clock she grew tired. She was used to going to bed early and even the short nap she had taken after dinner wasn't helping now. Where the heck was Ted? This was his shift, after all, and tomorrow at four-thirty in the morning she'd still have to do her own show.

Maybe coffee would help. As she stood up to dash out for a cup, Kyle walked in. "Hi, there. I just wanted to say that you're doing a great job."

"Thanks, but I'm about ready to go to sleep. I was going to fix myself a cup of strong coffee when you came in. Would you like some?"

"Sure would. To be honest, I'm tired myself. It's been a long day for me too." Kyle stuck his head out the doorway. "I hear the teletype machine going again. I'd better check on it."

Meg strode past him. "The booth will be okay for another seven minutes." She stepped out into the hall, Kyle right behind her. But she'd walked only a few feet when she heard the door of the booth click shut behind her. She spun around quickly. "Kyle, you didn't close the door, did you?"

His face paled. "Oh, my gawd! I'm so used to one of us being inside that I just forgot."

"Do you have the keys?"

"They're in my jacket—on the far side of the booth by the newscasters' mike."

"And to get there we have to open this door," Meg finished for him. "Of course, my keys are in my purse." She pointed. "There, next to my stool."

"First we get locked *in;* now we get locked *out.*" Kyle muttered an oath. "How much longer do we have before the cart machine runs out?"

"Six minutes."

"All right, follow me."

He ran down the hall, Meg at his heels. "Where are we going?" she asked.

"To the outside window."

"Kyle," she said, struggling for breath, "that's two stories up! How the heck are we going to climb up there?"

"Not *we,*" he corrected. *"You."*

Spring Madness 139

Her sides hurt as she gasped for air. "Are you crazy? I'm not about to try to scale a wall!"

"You won't have to. "I'll bring my car around, I'll stand on the hood, and you can stand on my shoulders."

They came to a stop right beneath the sound booth's window. "Have you gone completely out of your mind? We're Rager and Randall, a great radio team—not the Flying Worlycuts, world-renowned trapeze artists."

"Don't worry. I won't let you fall. If you start to lose your balance, I'll catch you." He dashed toward his car. "Stay there. I'll be right back."

Kyle parked his car directly beneath the window. "Okay," he said, scrambling onto the hood, "now you join me." He offered her a hand. "Then climb onto my shoulders."

"Kyle, the hood of your car won't take the strain, not to mention your shoulders."

"Meg, don't argue now. We're down to three minutes. Hurry."

Clearly, he wasn't going to take no for an answer. With a sigh Meg climbed onto the top of the car. Kyle squatted in front of her and she stepped precariously onto his shoulders. Kyle rose slowly, painfully, to his feet, almost losing his balance at one point, but recovering in the nick of time.

Meg swayed dangerously. "Easy, now!"

"I'm trying," he retorted.

As Kyle took a jerky step forward, Meg teetered violently. Suddenly her feet slipped out from under her, and she landed in a sitting position on his shoulders.

"Oomph!" she groaned.

"Be gentle with me," he called plaintively, almost staggering under her weight.

"Good grief, Kyle. That sounds like a line from one of those awful B movies," she teased.

He gripped both her hands firmly as she struggled to her feet once more. "Are you ready for me to let go yet?" he asked.

"Don't you dare. I'm going to keep holding on to one

of your hands while I reach toward the window. You're going to have to move forward a bit, though."

As Kyle inched toward the building, a loud police siren wailed right behind them, and a car came to a screeching halt. The sudden commotion almost made Meg lose her balance a second time.

She turned around slowly, afraid that any sudden movement would precipitate any number of disasters. "Now what?" she demanded.

"Put your hands up," an officer barked.

"He wants me to put my hands up at a time like this?" she muttered sarcastically.

"Officer, I can explain," Kyle said in a loud, clear voice. "I'm Kyle Rager. We're locked out of the radio station's control booth, and we've got to get back inside before the cart machine runs out."

"Kyle?" the officer exclaimed in astonishment.

"Joel, is that you?"

"Sure is, old buddy. What the hell are you up to?" He holstered his gun.

"This is the quickest way back inside the control booth—short of breaking down the door, which is reinforced with steel bars."

"How can you get into your sound booth through a window?" Joel asked. "I thought they had to have special sound-proofing insulation on all the walls."

"That's only with big studios nowadays. With good equipment and double-glazed windows, it's not really necessary. Anyway, radio personalities can't become claustrophobic. It's bad for business."

"Oh, boys," Meg called down sweetly, "do you think you could continue this chat later? I don't think I can hold up much longer." She leaned forward and grabbed the windowsill. "Kyle, I'm going to have to do a chin-up in order to reach," she said dejectedly, "and I've never been able to do a chin-up in my entire life!"

"Meg, try!"

"That's easy for you to say," she challenged. "You're down there."

"Believe me, being down here's no picnic either," Kyle retorted through clenched teeth.

The police officer stepped forward. "Kyle, I'm smaller than you are. If you think you can hold me, I know I could scramble onto that window."

"Give it a try, Joel, but hurry. I think my shoulders are sinking. Any time now they'll end up somewhere around my ankles."

Meg climbed down and the officer took her place. Within seconds he had raised the window and was inside.

Meg and Kyle ran around the building, then dashed up the stairs to the control booth. They halted in shocked surprise when Ted McCormick, looking like a bearded cherub, greeted them calmly from the console. Joel was standing at one side, a wide grin splitting his face.

"Boy, you can't trust anyone these days," Ted teased. "I arrive a little late and find that everyone's playing hooky and the station's broadcasting the swinging sounds of static. Tsk! Tsk! Then Joel, the lawman, comes in through the window and nearly scares me to death. Obviously this place falls apart without me."

Bedlam erupted as everyone began defending themselves against Ted's teasing charges. Seconds later they all stopped speaking abruptly and burst out laughing. Meg had never been so relieved in her life.

After thanking the policeman, who departed to resume his duties, Kyle and Meg retrieved their belongings and stepped into the hall.

Meg closed the door to the booth. "Remember this morning, when you told me I should learn to treat you as a friend, too? Well," she added, chuckling, "if this is what friends do together on their days off, I may not survive the relationship!"

"Why don't I buy you a drink?" Kyle suggested, leading the way to the parking lot. "After all, that's what good buddies do after a crisis."

"You're on," she agreed. "I think I've earned it."

Chapter 12

TWO WEEKS PASSED. Meg eagerly welcomed Kate's arrival back at Cabezon. The house just hadn't seemed the same without her. Meg's loneliness had reminded her that she simply wasn't cut out for a solitary life.

Kyle, aware of the isolation of Kate's house, had come over frequently. Sometimes he'd brought dinner for them to share. Other times he'd simply dropped by before going home at the end of a long workday. The fact that Kate's house was miles out of his way, and that working overtime was beginning to drain him of all his energy, never deterred him.

Meg worried about him. This week would be crucial for him, and she knew how concerned he was. His accounting books were scheduled to be presented to the bank on Friday. If the bank officials approved of KHAY's financial status, it would lend him the money necessary to buy a new transmitter. But if the bank didn't think he was qualified, his loan would be turned down, and he'd have to battle with their old transmitter for the foreseeable future, trying to keep it working.

In his effort to show that the station had indeed become a solid financial concern, he had worked practically around the clock gathering new sponsors and advertisers, as well as doing the engineering work needed on the equipment and broadcasting the morning show with her. Dark circles under his eyes attested to the strain he'd been under.

Kate placed a piece of apple crumb pie in front of Meg. "I'm worried about Kyle, Meg. He doesn't look well to me."

"He's been under a lot of pressure, Kate," she explained before sampling the dessert. "He needs a new transmitter soon because the old one's been breaking down with alarming frequency lately. If the bank doesn't approve his loan, it's going to be really difficult for him to compete with KLUV without an engineer there twenty-four hours a day to keep us on the air. Last week the transmitter went off several times. Granted, it was only for a total of a few minutes, but if an engineer hadn't been there to fix it, we could have lost a lot of programming. The more often we broadcast dead air, the less people are going to want to advertise through KHAY. We'll begin to look bad. Although the station's been breaking even lately, if Kyle's advertising revenue drops, he's going to be right back where he was months ago—on the verge of losing everything."

"So if the bank doesn't loan him the money, his station may not survive?" Kate paraphrased.

"That's about it. He needs to show that KHAY is on very solid ground, and that he's a good risk. To do that, he's been trying desperately to win new sponsors and to cut down on the overhead. The better his books look, the greater his chances of securing the loan."

"Is there anything we can do to help him?"

"I'm afraid it's out of our hands."

A knock sounded at the back door, and the next second Kyle walked in. "Hi, you two." He slumped into a chair at the table.

Spring Madness 145

Meg's heart went out to him. She could see the lines of exhaustion etched in his face, and his shoulders sagged with weariness. She fought a strong desire to take him upstairs to bed, undress him, and caress him to sleep.

"You look exhausted," Kate accused. "You haven't been taking care of yourself, have you? Kyle Rager, when's the last time you ate?"

"Lunch." He paused in thought. "No, breakfast." He paused again. "No, maybe it was dinner last night."

"That's what I thought," she said with a disapproving glare. "I'm going to fix you dinner right now." She pulled a steak out of the refrigerator.

"Aunt Kate, I'm really not hungry."

"No arguments," she said in a no-nonsense voice.

"What are you doing here?" Meg asked.

He smiled. "I wanted to make sure you were all right. I haven't had much chance to talk with you recently."

"You look so tired," she said softly.

"I am."

"Why didn't you just call me? It would have saved you a trip."

"I wanted to see you, Meg. You're important to me."

His concern touched her deeply. She reached for his hand and held it. "You're in no condition to drive all the way back to your house tonight, Kyle. If you try, you might end up falling asleep at the wheel."

"She's right," Kate agreed. "You can take the spare bedroom upstairs. There are already clean linens on the bed."

"I have to go home," he insisted. "I don't have my razor or clean clothes over here, and Meg and I have to be at the station at five A.M. tomorrow."

"I'll drive over to your place and get whatever you need," Meg volunteered. "Tonight you're going to stay here and let Kate and me take care of you."

"Maybe you're right," he conceded.

"Here." Meg placed a note pad and pencil before him. "Write down what you want me to bring."

"Now who's making demands?" he teased softly.

"But it makes all the difference in the world when they're based on—" She stopped abruptly. She had almost said *love*. "Genuine caring," she finished.

"So you've discovered that for yourself, have you?" He grinned.

"If you didn't look so pathetic right now," she teased, "I'd probably sock you in the nose for being so smug."

He rubbed the back of his neck with one hand. "Oh, by the way, some guy phoned for you this morning after you left. This afternoon he came by the station hoping to find you."

She frowned. "What guy?" she asked, thinking of Mike, then discarding the idea. Her ex-husband wouldn't have gone a block out of his way for her, let alone traverse an entire state. "Did he say who he was?"

"No, only that he'd call you at the station tomorrow after we finish our show." Kyle met her eyes. "I didn't tell him where you lived or what your telephone number was, since I wasn't sure what he wanted and he didn't leave a card with Patsy."

She twirled a strand of hair around her index finger. "I wonder who he is."

"I guess you'll find out tomorrow."

As Kate placed a plate and silverware before Kyle, Meg stood up. "I'm going to pick up your things while you're eating dinner." She smiled at Kate. "Take good care of him. He doesn't seem to be able to do a good job of that by himself."

"You two are ganging up on me," he complained, glancing hungrily toward the stove, where the steak was cooking.

By the time Meg returned, Kyle was sound asleep. Leaving a small suitcase filled with the items he had requested next to his door, she went to her own room. It felt strange to know that only one wall separated them. She stared at it wistfully, remembering what they had shared in the past.

With a sigh she undressed, switched off the lights,

and crawled between the sheets. That night she dreamed of a gentle, golden-haired knight who had stolen her heart.

She woke up slowly the following morning. Her sanity was fading quickly, she decided. What grown woman dreamed of knights and fantasy kingdoms and living happily ever after?

After dressing rapidly, she peeked into Kyle's room. His bed had already been made, and the suitcase was gone.

Kate greeted Meg as she entered the kitchen. "Kyle left for work already. He got up an hour ago. I heard him moving around, so I came down and fixed him a good breakfast. Now I'm going to do the same with you."

Recognizing the tone of Kate's voice, Meg realized that arguing would do no good.

A full hour later she arrived at the station, still feeling stuffed from the stack of pancakes Kate had prepared. As she entered the sound booth, she smiled at Kyle. "Boy, you're getting to be a real workaholic."

"I woke up shortly after three and couldn't get back to sleep. Do you realize that by the end of today I'll know if I've qualified for the loan on my transmitter?"

"And I'll find out who my mysterious caller is."

"You're not in some sort of trouble, are you?" he teased. "That guy sure looked like a federal investigator to me."

Meg laughed. "Darn, you've discovered my secret. I might as well confess that I'm wanted in several states."

Kyle laughed. "Ah, the refugee from KSUN in Phoenix. Your past is catching up to you, I see. Stairway to Heaven Crematorium has probably hired a hit man."

"Hide me," she pleaded, peering around furtively.

"Not me," He stepped away from her. "I believe in the old adage about women and children going first."

"That's not quite the way it goes."

Kyle laughed and handed her a script. "By the way, this is our household hints script for this morning's show."

Meg read it aloud. "'Shine It Up—How to Polish

Flatware, Jewelry, Silver, Copper, and Brass.'" She looked up. "Good one. This should get a good response from the listeners."

"I've already edited your copy of 'Nightly,' too, so if you're all set, let's go to the booth and get started."

"Wait a minute, let's see that one. You don't have any more not-so-subtle messages for me in today's episode, do you?" she demanded with a grin.

Straight-faced, he said, "Just a reference to women fugitives, I believe."

He ducked just in time to miss getting hit on the head with the script Meg was holding.

Toward the end of their show Meg received a short note from the receptionist that read:

> John Taylor left a message for you to call him during your next break. He said it's personal.

She didn't recognize the telephone number. Curiosity made her jumpy. Who was John Taylor? Taking a short break during a taped segment, she stepped out of the booth and went to a desk phone in the outer office. She never made personal calls on the listener lines.

She was connected to a local hotel room via a switchboard. The man who answered identified himself as John Taylor.

She didn't recognize his voice. "Hi, I'm Meg Randall," she said. "I received a message that you were looking for me."

"I sure was," the man began. "I represent radio station KBOY in Texas. Possibly you've heard of us. I'd like to talk to you. Do you have a few minutes?"

"That's about all I have," Meg explained apologetically. "I'm still on the air. But I'm familiar with your station. It has one of the largest listening audiences in the west. You have a fine reputation. What's this all about?"

"I'm here to offer you a job, Meg. Can I meet with

Spring Madness

you in person and explain the details?"

Meg's eyes widened in astonishment, but he certainly sounded sincere.

"How did you hear about me?" she asked suspiciously. "I've only been here for a short time."

"Luckily we managed to obtain a tape of several of your shows, and we liked what we heard," Taylor answered smoothly. "What do you say to meeting me to discuss the job offer?"

Meg considered only briefly before answering, "Thanks, but, no, thanks. I have a job, and I'm happy here."

"Don't make up your mind right away," he countered smoothly. "I'm prepared to offer a substantial increase in salary. Of course, I'm not certain what you make at KHAY, but I think our offer will probably be almost twice as much." The figure he mentioned was, indeed, extremely generous.

Meg's eyebrows rose. "You're kidding!"

"Not at all," he replied. "You're a valuable radio personality. Are you interested?"

"I don't know," she said hesitantly. The salary she was being offered was three times her current one, and working for a station like KBOY in Texas was bound to put her back at the top of her career field. KBOY was the largest station in the Southwest. "I'd have to think about it."

"It's a good offer," he pressed.

"I know. Believe me, I'm very tempted. But there are other considerations."

"I'm prepared to arrange some very good fringe benefits, should you accept our offer. In fact, I'd like to treat you to lunch and talk things over with you."

Meg glanced at her watch. "I've got to get back to the booth."

"Lunch, then?"

"All right," she agreed reluctantly. "How about one o'clock?"

"One it is."

"Meet me at the station at the receptionist's desk." She glanced at her watch again. "You'll have to excuse me, but I have to run."

After the show that morning she was walking with Kyle back to his office when T.J. greeted them in the hall. "Congratulations, Meg," he said. "I hear you've hit the big time. I overheard Patsy mention John Taylor's name when she took the call. He's the general manager of KBOY in Texas, isn't he? When I told Patsy who he was, it seems word just got around. I'm sorry if I was out of line."

"That's okay T.J.," Meg said. "What's a little scuttlebutt among friends?" It wouldn't help to be angry with him now. The damage was done. Darn it all! She had hoped to break the news to Kyle herself—very carefully.

"What was that all about?" Kyle asked.

"Remember the guy who's been asking for me?" Meg said. "His name is John Taylor, and he's from KBOY in Texas."

"What's he want?"

"He's here to offer me a job."

Kyle stopped walking. "What's he offering you?" He regarded her wearily.

"In short, more money and fringe benefits."

"Are you going to take it?"

"I don't think so."

"What's keeping you from accepting his offer outright?"

"Truthfully?" Meg gave him a level glance. "I like it here."

"Look, Meg, maybe I can make this easier for both of us. How much of a salary increase is he offering you? Once I get the loan for the transmitter, I won't need to be on such a tight budget. If all goes well..."

She told him what John Taylor had offered her.

Kyle whistled. "I could never match that."

"I know."

He resumed walking very slowly. "It would be your

chance to make it really big as a deejay. I can't offer you fame either. My station's too small."

In his office he closed the door behind them. "Meg, at one time you wanted to work solo, to make your way straight to the top and earn a name for yourself in this industry. This is your chance to do that. My station will never provide you with that kind of opportunity. As far as salary goes, I might manage a slight raise, but it may be years, maybe never, before I can even come close to what he's offering now." He shrugged. "Good grief, Meg, no three of us at the station put together make that much money!"

She smiled ruefully. "I know, Kyle, and I haven't asked you for a raise, have I?"

"No, you haven't," he conceded. "Still, I think you owe it to yourself to seriously consider KBOY's offer."

His reaction puzzled her. Why was he being so magnanimous? Didn't he want her to stay? The thought that he might be rejecting her struck deep within her heart. Just when she was beginning to think they might have a future together, he seemed to want to get rid of her. What was going on? "I'm having lunch with John Taylor," she told Kyle. "I'll see what else he has to say."

Kyle sat down at his desk and began sorting through a large stack of papers, his attention apparently not at all on her problem.

"I don't understand you," she said at length. "If you really value me and my work here, why are you taking this attitude?"

"What do you mean?" he asked, looking up.

"Why aren't you more upset at the prospect that I might be leaving? Doesn't it matter to you at all if I take the job and move away?"

He went over to her chair and pulled her up into his arms. His eyes bore into hers with burning intensity. "You mean a great deal to me, Meg. I think you know that. That's why I won't stand in your way. I can always travel to Texas and see you, if that's the way it turns out. But to keep you from doing what you want with your life"—

he held out his hands, palms up—"that isn't love, sweetheart. I care enough for you to let you become whatever you want to be."

He grazed her cheek tenderly with the back of his hand. "So if you're expecting me to pressure you one way or another, forget it. This is your decision." He smiled ruefully. "I'm no saint. I know what I *hope* you decide to do. But either way you and I will remain friends."

Meg left his office feeling more confused than ever before. Kyle's unselfishness had touched her deeply. It was exactly the kind of thing Mike would never have done for her.

She walked out of the station into the warm midday sun. Not long ago an offer like KBOY's would have sent her spirits soaring. Now it created a bothersome dilemma. Though the notion of tripling her salary was tempting, the thought of going anywhere without Kyle was too painful to contemplate. Like it or not, she was in love, and she'd never be happy working anyplace except by his side.

"Hi, Meg!" A familiar voice interrupted her thoughts, and she glanced up at a short, stylishly dressed businessman who must be John Taylor. "I recognized you from your promotional photos," he said. "They don't do you justice. Are you ready for lunch?"

Taking a deep breath, Meg turned to face him. "Mr. Taylor, I'm afraid I'm going to have to break our lunch date. You see, I've decided not to accept your offer."

"But you haven't even heard all of it yet!" he said, dismayed.

"That doesn't matter. KHAY more than fills my needs. I want to stay because I'm happy here. Money alone would never compensate for what I'd be losing if I left."

"That's your final decision?"

"I'm afraid it is." She shook hands with him. "I'm sorry."

"So am I," he replied. "If you ever change your mind, give me a call." He handed her his business card.

"I won't change my mind, but thanks, anyway."

Spring Madness

Meg walked back inside the station. Despite the fact that she had just turned down the offer of a lifetime, she felt elated and curiously relieved. Her priorities had certainly changed in the few weeks she had been working at KHAY. For the first time ever she was completely happy with her job, her home, and especially with Kyle.

As she entered the reception area, Patsy glanced up and said, "What are you doing here? Don't you remember you're supposed to meet John Taylor for lunch?"

Meg shrugged. "I saved him the trouble of taking me out."

Patsy leaned forward, her eyes bright. "Does that mean . . . ?"

"I turned him down," Meg confirmed. "I'm happy here, and that's too rare a feeling to trade for an increase in salary."

"You turned him down?" Kyle's voice rose slightly.

She turned to see him standing a few feet away. He had never looked better—tall, handsome, with earnest anticipation shimmering in his eyes. "Yes, I did."

With a loud whoop he sprang toward her, picked her up in his arms, and swung her around. "That's terrific!"

With a totally uninhibited squeal of delight, she wound her arms tightly around his neck. His obvious joy in her decision was worth all the money in the world.

Apparently hearing the commotion, the newscaster and the early afternoon deejay, who had just reported for work, hurried in to see what was happening. Suddenly aware that all eyes were on him, Kyle set Meg down abruptly. "Glad to have you back," he mumbled, then turned and strode back to his office.

Meg's eyes went from Patsy to the two men standing in the doorway. Biting her tongue to keep from laughing, she said straight-faced, "He's a very caring employer."

Loud laughter echoed behind her as she left the building to go get some lunch.

Chapter 13

MEG GLANCED NERVOUSLY at the crowd. Almost every seat in the bleachers of J. Edgar Hoover High School had been filled, and cars were still pulling into the parking lot. "I can't believe this crowd!" she exclaimed.

Kyle grinned exuberantly. "Isn't it terrific? The entire town has shown up for our softball game! And at fifty cents per ticket, our fund raising for the hospital children's ward is a sure success. First you decided to stick with me instead of taking that Texas job. Now we get this kind of turnout for our game. Nothing can beat me now, no matter what the final score."

"All that's true, but I'd still feel a lot better if I knew how to play softball," Meg replied dejectedly.

"Don't give it a thought," he said carelessly. "Patsy is one of the best softball players around. I used to play against her and her brothers, and let me tell you there's nothing she can't do. Between her and T.J., you'll be covered out in the field."

"Wrong," said T.J., approaching from behind. "Patsy's

155

sick with a bout of the stomach flu and can't come. Her sister Kathy is substituting for her and will play left field. And it looks like I'm going to have to cover for Ted, who was supposed to pitch. He's also got the flu. Someone else is going to have to play first base."

"But Ted's the best pitcher around for miles!" Kyle covered his face with one hand. "Meg, it looks like you're going to have to pull your own weight after all when we take the field. Do you think you can catch some of the fly balls and grounders that come your way, then throw the ball back to first or second base from the outfield?"

"Of course I can't!" she cried. A sinking feeling gnawed at her stomach as her eyes roamed over the huge crowd. Panic creeped over her. "Oh, I hope I don't make a fool out of myself in front of the entire town!" She looked hopefully up at the sky. "Could you all pray for rain, or perhaps a leftover horde of locusts?"

Kyle placed an arm around her shoulders. "You'll do fine," he assured her. "All you need is a little confidence."

"And a major miracle," said Monica Hanrahan with a chuckle as she joined the group. "Your team's already got problems, and the game hasn't even started yet. What's the matter, Kyle? Your people seem to be dropping like flies. Maybe you guys just don't get enough physical exercise to stay healthy."

Meg took note of Monica's designer blue jeans and bright red T-shirt with KLUV emblazoned in white across it. In contrast, Meg's old blue jeans and white shirt, which dated back to her college days, made her feel like one of the ugly stepsisters in *Cinderella*.

"And really, dear"—Monica turned to Meg—"you look a little peaked. Are you sure you're up to this?"

"Of course she is," Kyle answered for her.

Actually, Meg was about to agree with Monica and bow out, but obviously that was impossible now. "I'm going to try my best," she said, looking hopefully at the borrowed baseball glove on her left hand.

"That's the difference between us," Monica replied.

Spring Madness

"You try—I succeed." With a smug grin she turned and walked away.

"I suppose I should feel sorry for her," Meg said with a smirk. "With all that makeup on, she'll be too heavy to run the bases."

Kyle laughed. "I'd sure like to beat her today. She's such a sore loser, it would be her just deserts."

"Then I'll just have to do my best and not make any mistakes," Meg said. "But I warn you. My being on the field will probably be as helpful as tossing a cement block to a drowning man," she joked, trying to hide the fact that she was truly terrified. It was do-or-die time. "You should have let me quit when Monica asked about my health," she added. "It was the perfect way out, and our team would have been better off without me."

"I couldn't have replaced you even if I wanted to, Meg," Kyle said. "We need nine players to stay in the game. Fortunately the relatives of some of our staff have volunteered. With you, that gives us the required nine."

"I think they want you at home plate, Kyle," T.J. said, joining them. "Coach Higgins, the umpire, is getting ready for the coin toss."

"The what?" Meg felt as if she had just entered a foreign country.

"Whoever wins the toss gets to be the home team. They take the field first and bat last," T.J. explained.

"That doesn't make sense. Why wouldn't they want to bat first?"

"It's called the home-team advantage. That gives them the last chance to score at the end of each inning," Kyle explained.

"Oh." Meg swallowed. "Why are sports so darned hard to understand?"

"Don't worry about the details," T.J. advised. "You know how to put someone out, and Kyle says you can hit the ball. You have the glove on the correct hand, and you can tell first base from third. That's all you need to know."

"All right," she said with determination. "If I'm going

to do this, then I'll do it right and give it everything I've got."

Kyle won the coin toss and led their team onto the field, getting the game off to a good start. "We've assigned you to play right field, Meg," he said. "It should be a little easier because, on the average, fewer balls are hit there. Just do your best." He winked at her assuringly, then ran over to his own position in center field.

Monica was the first batter up for the KLUV team. "Hey, T.J.," she goaded the pitcher, "chased any fire trucks lately?"

Meg could tell from the laughter coming from KLUV's team bench that part of Monica's strategy was to do whatever it took to distract KHAY's pitcher. Monica's barb, shot just when T.J. was winding up to pitch, made him hesitate infinitesimally. The ball he threw bounced to home plate. Kyle groaned as a laugh went up from the crowd.

"Just throw the ball in there, T.J.," Kyle encouraged him. "Don't listen to a word she says."

T.J. gave Monica a cold glare. His shoulders squared as he stared at the catcher's signals. Determination was etched in his brow.

Three pitches later, Monica walked back to her team bench fuming, having struck out. Encouraged, Meg joined KHAY's team as it urged its pitcher on with loud cheers. "T.J., KHAY, all the way!" The players chanted when every opponent came to the plate.

The game proceeded for another couple of innings, with both teams scoring a run each time at bat. In the top half of the third inning, a KLUV player hit the ball with a loud thump, sending it sailing toward Meg. She held her breath. This was her chance. She dashed forward, trying to catch it in midair, but her feet got tangled, and she went careening forward onto her knees. Swearing softly, she stumbled to her feet.

The ball had hit the ground and was rolling toward her. Scrambling madly forward, she scooped it up and threw it to second base as quickly as she could.

Spring Madness

The play hadn't really required much exertion, but she felt as if she had just run a marathon. Her heart was pumping furiously as she returned to her position in right field. It was such a curse to be clumsy!

But when Kyle yelled out at her, "Hey, lady, good play," she felt immensely reassured. His words warmed her through and through, and she smiled back. Now if she could only survive the rest of the game. She looked around. What was a nice sports-hating girl like her doing in a place like this, anyway?

Meg's worst nightmares became reality in the bottom half of the third inning. The score was tied at three-three, and it was her turn to bat. Time to be a heroine she told herself over and over again. She pictured herself hitting a home run, and the crowd cheering. Concentrating on that mental picture, she stood next to home plate and took several practice swings. It felt as natural as swatting bugs with a tennis racket.

Meg kept her eyes on the ball, then swung the bat, putting all her strength into it. She actually hit the ball! But as she ran toward first base, she saw the pitcher catch the ball in midair. The umpire's voice rang loudly in her ears as he called the play. She was out.

Dejectedly she walked back to the bench and met her teammates.

"Don't let it bother you. You did fine, Meg," Kyle said quietly, placing an arm around her shoulders. "You hit it farther than Monica did."

She smiled. "By golly, you're right." She nodded, feeling considerably cheered up. "Thanks."

He winked. "Don't worry about it. Like they say, there's always next time."

"That certainly has an ominous ring to it," she muttered.

Unfortunately she didn't fare much better the next time she was up at bat. This time the ball sailed straight up into the sky. As it came spinning back to earth, the catcher easily caught it. Once again she had failed to get on base.

The rest of the team was doing well, though, much

better than expected. When they entered the last inning, KHAY was ahead, seven–six.

Meg concentrated as Kyle coached from his position in center field, though she kept reminding herself that balls were seldom hit in her direction. Her complacency was shattered when the first KLUV batter hit a line drive just over first base. Like a bullet the ball sailed past her on her left. She sprinted toward it, but the ball bounced off the ground, then, to her dismay, arched right over her head.

Whirling like a dust devil, Meg spun on her heels. She was still trying to reach the ball when Kyle leaped into the air, snagged the ball in his glove, and hurled it back toward second base.

The crowd cheered, and Kyle's teammates praised his quick action. "Way to go, Kyle!" T.J. shouted. "You kept him from getting extra bases on that one."

Kyle grinned, not even winded by the effort. "I told you I'd back you up, Meg," he said. "And before you get too discouraged, remember that line drives are hard for anyone to stop."

Meg grimaced.

The inning dragged on. Meg checked her wristwatch often, beginning to wonder if she'd died and gone to hell and was serving time by playing in an endless baseball game. After a series of pitches and foul balls that seemed to take forever, the next batter struck out.

"One down, two to go," Kyle called out to his team.

Meg's eyes came to rest on Monica as she stepped up to the plate, ready to bat. At least there was one consolation. Monica's day had been as frustrating as her own. Meg exhaled softly. Well, perhaps that wasn't entirely accurate. Monica had caught a few ground and fly balls when she'd been playing outfield.

"Move in closer!" Kyle yelled to Kathy, their left fielder. To Meg he added, "She can't hit it out of the infield."

Relieved, Meg watched as Monica made it to first base safely with a walk. At least Meg had been spared

Spring Madness

trying to scramble for a ball determined to elude her. Now, if only the rest of the game would go by smoothly, she might be able to avoid further embarrassment. Surely that wasn't too much to hope for.

Meg remained close behind the first baseman, forgetting to move back into position as the next player came to the plate. With a loud crack the ball shot directly at her. Instinctively she put her hand in front of her face, and an instant later something hard thumped into her glove, stinging her hand.

Realizing that by some miracle she had managed to catch the ball, she reached out quickly with her right hand and grabbed the ball before it fell.

Kyle was running up from behind her, shouting something. "Tag Monica!" he yelled. "She's off base!"

Monica was directly in front of Meg, standing about halfway between first and second base, obviously as confused as Meg about the sudden change of events. A cacophony of sound engulfed them as everyone yelled conflicting directions.

Somehow Meg heard Kyle's voice above the din. Focusing on what he was saying, she tried to cut Monica off before she could dart back to safety. With a yelp Monica tried to dodge Meg. She frantically dove toward the base, but at that instant Meg lunged forward. Reaching as far as she could, she jumped toward Monica, holding the ball in a white-knuckled death grip.

When the dust cleared, Monica was lying on the ground, sputtering, first base just beyond the grasp of her outstretched arms.

Kyle picked Meg up, pulled her into a powerful bear hug, and twirled her around ecstatically. "You did it, Meg! A double play! We've won!"

"Don't we bat now?" Meg asked, thoroughly confused.

"We don't have to. We were already ahead. The game's over, sweetheart. We've won!" he repeated.

Elated by this sudden change of events, Meg cheered along with her teammates, who had joined them and were slapping each other on the back. "All the way with K-HAY-HAY," the team chanted, and Meg joined right in with the other players.

A moment later the crowd was coming toward them, their fans vacating the bleachers and streaming onto the playing field.

"Way to go, Kyle," a man cheered. "Who'd have thought our town's favorite son and his new partner would save the game!"

Meg beamed.

The crowd milled about them, trapping the entire team in the middle. Caps and gloves were tossed into the air as praise flowed from all sides.

"You two are the best thing that's happened to this town," a voice told them from off to their right.

"I still can't believe how many people showed up for the game," Kyle said, grinning from ear to ear.

"We support what you're trying to do, buddy." Joel, his policeman friend, offered his hand. "Your station's really helping this community pull together."

The high school coach who had acted as their umpire reached the official's table and turned on the loudspeaker. "Folks, our volunteers have just informed me that this game has collected even more money than we anticipated. We have enough to buy color television sets for the children's ward, as well as the funds to replace the old furniture in the parents' waiting room."

A loud cheer went up, and more congratulations came pouring in. Several parents came by to thank Kyle and Meg personally. Though embarrassed by the effusive praise, Meg felt elated with the sense of community spirit that had drawn Kyle back to Cabezon.

It was a wonderful feeling to be part of this town. For the first time she realized just what it was that bound Kyle to the people.

An individual whom they both recognized as the station's banker pushed his way toward them. "Congratulations on your victory," he said, presenting his hand to shake. "Your station is becoming a real asset to the community." He stepped forward and whispered briefly in Kyle's ear, then excused himself.

"What did he say, Kyle?" Meg asked, pulling him toward the far side of the bleachers so that they could steal a private moment together. "Was it about the loan?"

"As a matter of fact, yes. He apologized for not giving me an answer the other day."

"Well, did we get the loan or not?" she demanded impatiently.

"Yes," Kyle murmured. *"We* did." His arms curved around her waist as his lips brushed hers in a light kiss. "Thank you, sweetheart, for coming into my life," he whispered.

"You're a very special man, Kyle Rager," she replied. But her words were lost as the crowd clamored around them once again.

Chapter 14

MEG STOOD NEXT to Kyle and the soft-drink stand. The public continued to mill around them, asking their opinion on everything from the purchase of livestock to the upcoming bond issue. Meg was running on nervous energy; just beneath her exuberance lay exhaustion. As she was discussing the possibility of Rager and Randall's doing a live broadcast from the high school during its spring dance, she caught sight of Monica Hanrahan coming toward them.

Her face was pinched, but she managed to produce a thin smile. "Congratulations on behalf of KLUV, Kyle," she said, extending her hand.

Kyle accepted it. "I can't believe we won!"

"Neither can I," Monica replied dryly.

Meg started to laugh, but bit her tongue and turned away to hide her amusement. This was Kyle's moment of glory, and she didn't want to distract him in any way. Instead, Meg stood quietly and watched.

"Look at it this way, Monica," Kyle said. "It all went for a good cause."

"That's true," she replied. "But I still think you lucked out."

"It looks like KHAY has managed to hold its own in the competition against KLUV," Kyle taunted, leaning back against the soft-drink stand and regarding her with an air of cool superiority.

"Yes. Who'd have thought it?" she mumbled.

Meg could tell that it was taking all of Monica's willpower not to lose her temper in front of the gathered crowd. Kyle however, continued to tease her unmercifully. "You've tried, though," he said, "and that's the important thing. Like Meg told you earlier, knowing you've done your best is all you can expect from yourself."

Monica pursed her lips. "I may have lost this round, Kyle," she said too sweetly to be sincere, "but KLUV is still the number one station around here, and I'm going to see that it stays that way. Don't let this victory make you complacent. We've each won a battle, but the war's far from over."

"We'll take it one day at a time," he agreed. "So far it's worked, and I don't believe in changing a winning game." He stood with his feet slightly apart, his hands jammed into his pockets, and stared at her arrogantly.

Monica nodded, then abruptly took Meg's arm and led her away from the crowd. Caught off guard, Meg went along without protest.

Once they stood apart from the others, Monica smiled. "I heard you turned down KBOY's offer."

Meg's eyebrows shot up in surprise. "That's right, but how did you know?"

"I taped one of your shows and sent it to a friend. He's the owner of the station," she answered matter-of-factly. Narrowing her eyes speculatively, she studied Meg silently for several seconds. "What I don't understand is why you didn't take the job. You're making a big mistake."

"I don't think so," Meg replied coldly. The thought that Monica had attempted to manipulate her was making her seethe. "In fact, now that I know it was a phony offer, I'm doubly glad I turned it down."

Monica shrugged. "It was on the level. I piqued their interest, but in the end it was your tape that sold them. There's probably still time to change your mind, if you want to."

"I don't," Meg replied flatly. "Why did you promote me to KBOY anyway? Am I interfering with your plans for Kyle?"

"Something like that. You're very good at your job, though I'll never admit that in front of anyone else. Your teaming up with Kyle has put KHAY back into contention, and it's upset my plans—only temporarily, of course.

"You're giving up a great deal, Meg," Monica continued. "What's happened to your ambition? Are you sure Kyle's worth it? His life's not going anywhere. He's perfectly happy managing and owning his little station. He won't ever amount to much with that kind of philosophy." Monica's complexion glowed with anger and impatience. "By sticking with him, you're dooming yourself to a similar fate."

"There was a time when I thought that nothing was more important than getting to the top of my field," Meg answered. "But that's not the case anymore. Priorities, like everything else in life, change." To her surprise, she found herself feeling sorry for Monica.

"And you're certain that years from now you won't look back on what you gave up and resent Kyle for it?" Monica's eyes gleamed with maliciousness.

"I'm sure. Like most people, what I'm really looking for in my life is happiness. Once, I believed that my career would provide that. Now I've found something that's infinitely better."

Kyle appeared from around the corner. "I couldn't help but overhear, ladies," he explained. "I went to talk to Higgins about the live broadcast he wants KHAY to do from the gym, when I heard my name being mentioned." He gazed anxiously at Meg. "As much as I hate to admit it, Monica's got a point. Are you sure that staying here is what will make you happy?"

"I'm absolutely certain," she replied, her hands tingling as she fought the urge to reach out to him.

"How touching," Monica said, rolling her eyes. "And how revolting."

"Monica, take a close look at yourself," Kyle advised. "And not just at your tangled hair and smudged makeup. You're carving out a very lonely future for yourself by placing more value on money than on friendship. Make sure that's what you want before it's too late to turn back."

"How quaint! Who'd have thought you'd take up preaching as a hobby!" she retorted, her tone dripping with sarcasm. Turning on her heels, she stomped away.

An hour later, after all the borrowed baseball equipment had been returned to the staff of J. Edgar Hoover High School, Meg walked with Kyle back to the parking lot. "I don't think I'll ever forget today for as long as I live," she said.

Kyle laughed. "Me neither. How's it feel to know you saved the game?"

She shook her head. "That's really not very important in comparison to what I learned about you and the people here today. This is a very special community, Kyle."

"Yes, it is." He opened the car door for her. "Why don't you let me fix you a drink over at my home? It's not far from here, and it will be hours before the celebration party at Aunt Kate's begins." His eyes met hers in intimate communication. "This has been such a fantastic day. I want to share the afternoon with you. After all, you're the one who made it happen for me." He chuckled. "I'd have given anything to capture the moment when Monica got angry at us for caring more about each other than for the almighty dollar."

Meg laughed, too. "Still, Kyle, you shouldn't have been so blunt. I thought for a minute that she was going

Spring Madness 169

to slap you instead of walking away."

"She's been a constant thorn in my side these past few months," Kyle mused icily. "I thought it was time I confronted her with the truth about herself."

"She's a formidable adversary, yet you managed to hold your own against her and her checkbook. Today your success was complete when you got the loan you needed from the bank. I must admit I'm impressed. Do you realize that you've done everything you set out to do? KHAY is now an established part of this community."

"I didn't do it alone, Meg," he said candidly. "Part of this victory belongs to you, too." He paused. Then he added, "So, how about it? Will you come over to my place and celebrate with me?"

Meg knew that Kyle accepted her as both a woman and as a professional. The knowledge filled her with pride. She began to share the thought, then stopped, realizing there was no need to explain. A gentle rush of love and affection coursed through her.

"I'd be delighted," she said simply.

Until now, Meg had planned to relax before the party that evening, but the thought of spending time alone with Kyle revitalized her energy.

Twenty minutes later she met him at the entrance to his house. She followed him inside and waited in the living room.

"I had this chilled just for the occasion," he said, returning with a bottle of champagne. "I bought a case for the party tonight, but it won't hurt if we're one bottle short."

"Cocky, aren't you?" she teased.

Kyle struggled with the cork. Suddenly, without warning, it popped loudly out of the bottle and bounced harmlessly off the ceiling. The foamy, bubbly liquid spurted all over them.

"I'm sorry," he said quickly, turning the bottle toward the fireplace and allowing the overflow to spurt inside the grate.

Meg pulled her wet clothes away from her body. "Champagne and dirt! What a combination."

"You need a bath," he said, his eyes drifting over her in a slow, lingering appraisal, finally coming to rest on her slender hips.

She smiled. "So do you." She circled his waist with her arms and looked up into his face.

"Are you thinking what I'm thinking?" he asked huskily.

"Two minds with but a single thought," she replied.

He began to unbutton her white cotton top, but Meg stepped back. "We're not even near the shower yet," she said, laughing.

"Are you afraid to stand naked before me, here, in the full light of day?" he drawled.

In answer she lifted both her hands to her buttons and began unfastening them one by one.

Kyle took a step toward her, but she moved back. Unclasping her jeans, then slipping out of her undergarments, she stood brazenly before him, confident in the knowledge that they belonged to each other.

Kyle came toward her, his eyebrows raised. "I never know just what to expect from you." He pulled her into his arms, his hunger for her a hot and heady elixir that made her blood boil. "If you tease me like this, we may not make it to that shower until later—much later," he growled in her ear.

"There's no need to rush," she said in a soft, seductive voice. "A little patience can heighten the pleasure." She undressed him slowly, enjoying the feel of his naked flesh beneath her fingertips. "You're so masculine," she whispered. "It makes me glad that I'm a woman."

"I love you, Meg," he said in a throaty voice that seemed to be torn from the depths of his soul. He pulled her to him, crushing her mouth, tasting the delicate outline of her lips.

The wild need that drove him communicated itself to her, drawing her heart to him. "I love you, Kyle."

He tore his lips from the hollow of her throat, pushing

away to look into her eyes. "Meg, do you know what you just said?"

She nodded. "I love you, Kyle.' She felt like shouting the words from his rooftop.

"Then there's no escape for either of us. We're a team on and off the air, because now that you've said it, there'll be no turning back."

With a sigh she buried her head against his chest. "Let's go take a long, hot shower," she said.

"Yes, let's." He lifted her against his body and ravaged her parted lips, his tongue plundering the moist, sweet regions beyond.

Meg quivered as his aroused manhood pressed against her. While his arms imprisoned her waist, she willingly lifted her hips against him, her senses spinning and swirling as the world retreated, giving way to a reality where only pleasure ruled. His superior male strength, the feel of his hair-roughened chest so intimately molded against hers, made her body turn liquid with desire.

He carried her as if she weighed no more than a feather and lifted her into the shower enclosure, following seconds later. Adjusting the nozzle, he allowed the steaming liquid to assault their bodies.

The spray stung them as their mouths met in a hungry reunion. Despite its heat, the water seemed cold in comparison to the warmth radiating from the very core of her being. Droplets beaded on Kyle's chest, then joined those on her own flesh before cascading to the porcelain tiles.

"This is the way I want you, Meg—holding nothing back, completely mine."

"What an easy wish to fulfill," she murmured.

He cupped a breast in one hand, the rosy center taut with the passion he had kindled. Lowering his mouth to it, he caressed it gently with the tip of his tongue. Meg shivered with the electric sensations the contact produced, and her body went limp against his. Kyle's arms supported her as he continued to assault her senses.

His mouth plundered hers. Then just when she swore

that the universe itself converged in that kiss, he curved his hands around her buttocks and presed her against his hardened flesh. She felt the fervor of an all-encompassing pleasure as he entered her slowly, infusing her spirit with a wild, pulsating need.

With each ragged breath she strove to join herself to him. As his maleness engulfed her, she acknowledged the potent aphrodisiac her femininity was to Kyle. Theirs was a love between two equals who sought more for the other than for themselves. It was the culmination of all her fantasies.

The sure knowledge fueled the passion that singed their bodies and souls with love's pure white flame.

With a helpless moan she offered all of herself to him. In a blaze of unequaled passion, they were lifted beyond the boundaries of the flesh and soared to a universe of dreams...

Long moments later, Kyle moved her beneath the gentle, flowing water. Tenderly he rinsed her body off, then allowed her to do the same for him.

"Of course, now there's only one thing left to do," he said seriously.

"You want me to serve you hand and foot by going to get the towels," she said with mock resignation.

Kyle laughed as he stepped out of the shower. "No." His expression grew serious again. "Meg"—he wrapped one of the towels around her and pulled her against him—"marry me."

The words shocked her.

She had come to terms with the fact that she loved him and marriage was the next logical step, she supposed. But a familiar dread chilled the blood that had coursed through her with such heated warmth just minutes before.

"I don't know," she said, stiffening and pulling away.

"You're in love with me, Meg. What could be more natural?"

"I have to think, Kyle." The words sounded high-pitched and came too fast. "And I have to do that somewhere away from you."

Spring Madness

Her towel around her, she went to the living room. Meg picked up her clothes from the floor and dressed quickly.

Kyle followed her, wearing a robe. His hair was tousled and damp, but she had never seen him look more breathtakingly virile.

"You're running away again," he noted ruefully.

"Not really. I'll be with you at Kate's in a few hours for the victory celebration. Just give me a little time to think about what you've said. A lot has happened lately, in both of our lives."

He stood very still, his gaze running over her features in a lengthy assessment.

She didn't want him to sense her panic. It would hurt him terribly, and that was the last thing she wanted. Trying to reassure him, she kissed him lightly. "Kyle, I do love you. Please believe that."

Not giving him a chance to answer, she hurried out the front door.

Meg drove aimlessly for a long time. Marriage? Kyle was making an impossible demand. She'd barely adjusted to the fact that she loved him...

Demands. Relationships seemed to be filled with them. She had grown to realize that Kyle's demands stemmed from love, not from selfishness. But they were demands just the same. Could she fulfill his needs without sacrificing her own?

Maybe her greatest need *was* to give to Kyle. The alternative was never to make a commitment, and thereby lose him. No man would wait forever.

Her mind whirled in confusion. Her thoughts ran full circle, ending up where they had started, with the same unanswered questions. Perhaps what she needed was a diversion. The party wouldn't begin for a couple of hours. Remembering that the script for the latest episode of "Nightly" needed final revision, Meg headed for the station.

She parked near the rear entrance. Using her key, she

entered the building and walked to Kyle's office. But the script wasn't there. She searched the entire room but couldn't find it. Out of desperation she opened Kyle's top drawer. As she did, her eyes came to rest on a small rectangular box. A small card with her name on it had been attached to it.

She stared at it. It wasn't hers to open, but it did have her name on it. Surely there wouldn't be any harm in taking a peek...

Was she just making excuses for something she knew she shouldn't do? Of course she was! But suddenly she had to know what was in that box!

She carefully lifted the lid. In the center lay a gold heart, the twin to the one she and Kyle had buried for their treasure hunt. But this one, had a different inscription:

To Meg, the lady who stole my heart.

KYLE

Meg recalled the first time she had seen the two hearts at the Santa Fe goldsmith's shop. She had raved about them, wishing she could have purchased the remaining one. Kyle had remembered, and had obviously gone back and bought it for her as a token of his love.

The gesture touched her deeply. Meg sat down in Kyle's chair, recalling the events of the past few months. With sudden, alarming clarity she realized that his demands would not be demands at all. They'd be a part of what she'd give freely because of her love for him.

Feeling as if a great weight had been lifted from her shoulders, and happy that her course of action was clear at last, she leaned back in his chair and closed her eyes.

The resounding crash of breaking glass woke her up. Sitting up abruptly, she saw that the sun was visible just above the windowsill.

Meg gasped. She had slept all night in Kyle's chair

Spring Madness

and missed their victory celebration! Glancing at her watch, she muttered an oath. Not only that, but she had managed to miss the first fifteen minutes of their show. By now Kyle must be furious.

Meg dashed to the door. Ignoring Patsy, who was busy picking up the remnants of a shattered coffee mug from the floor, she ran through the reception area at full speed.

She arrived at the booth out of breath seconds later. Kyle was addressing their listeners. "And here she is, ladies and gentlemen"—he eyed her suspiciously—"looking as bright and fresh as a wilted daisy. What the heck happened to you?"

Meg put on her headphones, then switched on her microphone. "After you thoroughly confused me last night, I went for a long drive."

"And you slept in my office," he finished.

"How did you know?"

"When you failed to show up for the party, I called the nighttime deejay. He saw your car in the parking lot, so I knew you were here somewhere. I peeked in this morning, but you looked so peaceful I decided not to wake you. What were you doing in there, anyway?"

"Being the devoted employee I am, I came back to the office to pick up some work."

"I'm impressed."

"You should be."

"Then what?"

"I was looking for our script of 'Nightly.' After searching the entire office without any luck, I decided to look in your desk."

"I see. You were being nosy," he countered good-naturedly.

"I found your heart."

Kyle laughed. "Lady, you've had it all along."

"Folks, let me tell you about the present this wonderful man bought for me," she said. She recounted the story of how they had found the two hearts, and how she hadn't had the money to purchase the remaining one.

"But I don't understand," Kyle said. "If you found it,

and if you liked it as much as you say, why aren't you wearing it now?"

"I don't want to be pushy. I thought I'd wait until you gave the heart to me—officially, that is."

"You're nosy, but honest," he quipped.

"I'm glad you appreciate my virtues."

Patsy walked into the sound booth and handed Kyle the box. "Folks, our secretary, who also goes through my desk"—he gave Patsy a wink—"has just brought me the heart. I want you all to be witnesses. I am now officially placing this around Meg's neck."

"It sounds like strangulation," Meg shot back. "Try a little sweet talk, Romeo."

"For that I need help. How about you people out there giving me a hand? What can I say to Meg that will sweep her off her feet?"

"Tell her you're madly in love with her," one caller suggested.

"Tell her she's the heart of your life," said another.

Kyle and Meg both groaned.

"Tell her she means everything to you," a third caller suggested.

Kyle looked at her, his eyes never wavering. "Would any of those work?"

"I like most what you said to me yesterday."

Kyle's features softened with understanding.

"How about repeating the question?" she suggested. "It's one that never sounds trite, no matter how many times it's been said before."

Kyle reached across the booth and held her hand. "Will you marry me?"

Meg swallowed. "Yes."

"If you'll excuse us for just a moment," Kyle told the listeners. He removed his headset, then gently pulled off hers. He stood up and, offering his hand, helped her to her feet. "So the team of Rager and Randall ends."

"But the partnership of Rager and Rager is just beginning."

Then his mouth was on hers, hot, demanding, and

indescribably tender. "I love you," he told her again and again as he covered her face with kisses.

Meg fitted herself against the hard length of his body. "I'll do everything I can to make you happy, Kyle, I promise."

"You already have," he said thickly.

"This is sweet," said T.J., interrupting on the newscasters' microphone, "but do you realize you're broadcasting over the air? I hate to ruin this tender moment, but the whole town's listening."

Meg stared aghast at the live microphone. Before she could recover, however, the switchboard lights all began to glow.

"And now for the grand finale, folks," Kyle informed their listeners. "T.J.'s going to take over for us and start his shift early. My bride-to-be and I have wedding plans to make."

As music filled the airwaves, Kyle again took Meg in his arms. "Where were we?" he murmured as his lips covered hers.

Second Chance at Love

___ 0-425-08200-8	LOVE PLAY #269 Carole Buck	$2.25
___ 0-425-08201-6	CAN'T SAY NO #270 Jeanne Grant	$2.25
___ 0-425-08202-4	A LITTLE NIGHT MUSIC #271 Lee Williams	$2.25
___ 0-425-08203-2	A BIT OF DARING #272 Mary Haskell	$2.25
___ 0-425-08204-0	THIEF OF HEARTS #273 Jan Mathews	$2.25
___ 0-425-08284-9	MASTER TOUCH #274 Jasmine Craig	$2.25
___ 0-425-08285-7	NIGHT OF A THOUSAND STARS #275 Petra Diamond	$2.25
___ 0-425-08286-5	UNDERCOVER KISSES #276 Laine Allen	$2.25
___ 0-425-08287-3	MAN TROUBLE #277 Elizabeth Henry	$2.25
___ 0-425-08288-1	SUDDENLY THAT SUMMER #278 Jennifer Rose	$2.25
___ 0-425-08289-X	SWEET ENCHANTMENT #279 Diana Mars	$2.25
___ 0-425-08461-2	SUCH ROUGH SPLENDOR #280 Cinda Richards	$2.25
___ 0-425-08462-0	WINDFLAME #281 Sarah Crewe	$2.25
___ 0-425-08463-9	STORM AND STARLIGHT #282 Lauren Fox	$2.25
___ 0-425-08464-7	HEART OF THE HUNTER #283 Liz Grady	$2.25
___ 0-425-08465-5	LUCKY'S WOMAN #284 Delaney Devers	$2.25
___ 0-425-08466-3	PORTRAIT OF A LADY #285 Elizabeth N. Kary	$2.25
___ 0-425-08508-2	ANYTHING GOES #286 Diana Morgan	$2.25
___ 0-425-08509-0	SOPHISTICATED LADY #287 Elissa Curry	$2.25
___ 0-425-08510-4	THE PHOENIX HEART #288 Betsy Osborne	$2.25
___ 0-425-08511-2	FALLEN ANGEL #289 Carole Buck	$2.25
___ 0-425-08512-0	THE SWEETHEART TRUST #290 Hilary Cole	$2.25
___ 0-425-08513-9	DEAR HEART #291 Lee Williams	$2.25
___ 0-425-08514-7	SUNLIGHT AND SILVER #292 Kelly Adams	$2.25
___ 0-425-08515-5	PINK SATIN #293 Jeanne Grant	$2.25
___ 0-425-08516-3	FORBIDDEN DREAM #294 Karen Keast	$2.25
___ 0-425-08517-1	LOVE WITH A PROPER STRANGER #295 Christa Merlin	$2.25
___ 0-425-08518-X	FORTUNE'S DARLING #296 Frances Davies	$2.25
___ 0-425-08519-8	LUCKY IN LOVE #297 Jacqueline Topaz	$2.25
___ 0-425-08626-7	HEARTS ARE WILD #298 Janet Gray	$2.25
___ 0-425-00627-5	SPRING MADNESS #299 Aimée Duvall	$2.25
___ 0-425-08628-3	SIREN'S SONG #300 Linda Barlow	$2.25
___ 0-425-08629-1	MAN OF HER DREAMS #301 Katherine Granger	$2.25
___ 0-425-08630-5	UNSPOKEN LONGINGS #302 Dana Daniels	$2.25
___ 0-425-08631-3	THIS SHINING HOUR #303 Antonia Tyler	$2.25

Prices may be slightly higher in Canada.

Available at your local bookstore or return this form to:

SECOND CHANCE AT LOVE
Book Mailing Service
P.O. Box 690, Rockville Centre, NY 11571

Please send me the titles checked above. I enclose _____. Include 75¢ for postage and handling if one book is ordered; 25¢ per book for two or more not to exceed $1.75. California, Illinois, New York and Tennessee residents please add sales tax.

NAME_____

ADDRESS_____

CITY_____ STATE/ZIP_____

(allow six weeks for delivery)

SK-41b

COMING NEXT MONTH IN THE SECOND CHANCE AT LOVE SERIES

THE FIRE WITHIN #304 by Laine Allen
Ecstasy turns to rage, tenderness to torment, when Cara Chandler's secrets...and Lou Capelli's suspicions...twist their whirlwind marriage into a sham of wedded bliss!

WHISPERS OF AN AUTUMN DAY #305 by Lee Williams
Adam Brady has "stolen" her famous grandfather's love letters, and Lauri Fields *must* get them back—no matter what deceptive... or seductive...measures she must take!

SHADY LADY #306 by Jan Mathews
Catherine Coulton intends to arrest the man for solicitation—instead she finds herself locked in his hungry embrace! Then she learns he's Nick Samuels, infamous womanizer...*and* celebrated vice-squad cop!

TENDER IS THE NIGHT #307 by Helen Carter
Popular Toni Kendall clashes with possessive Chris Carpenter from their first explosive encounter—though his take-charge manner attests to a strength she can't resist!

FOR LOVE OF MIKE #308 by Courtney Ryan
Hours after jilting her fiancé, Gabby Cates is stranded on a deserted beach in a bedraggled wedding gown, with her cat, her guilty conscience...and slightly intoxicated, thoroughly spellbinding Mike Hyatt...

TWO IN A HUDDLE #309 by Diana Morgan
Dynamite quarterback Trader O'Neill knows all the right moves. But Selena Derringer, reluctant owner of the *worst* football team wonders if he's offering a lasting commitment or merely masterful game playing...

QUESTIONNAIRE

1. How do you rate _____
   (please print TITLE)
   - ☐ excellent
   - ☐ very good
   - ☐ good
   - ☐ fair
   - ☐ poor

2. How likely are you to purchase another book in this series?
   - ☐ definitely would purchase
   - ☐ probably would purchase
   - ☐ probably would not purchase
   - ☐ definitely would not purchase

3. How likely are you to purchase another book by this author?
   - ☐ definitely would purchase
   - ☐ probably would purchase
   - ☐ probably would not purchase
   - ☐ definitely would not purchase

4. How does this book compare to books in other contemporary romance lines?
   - ☐ much better
   - ☐ better
   - ☐ about the same
   - ☐ not as good
   - ☐ definitely not as good

5. Why did you buy this book? (Check as many as apply)
   - ☐ I have read other SECOND CHANCE AT LOVE romances
   - ☐ friend's recommendation
   - ☐ bookseller's recommendation
   - ☐ art on the front cover
   - ☐ description of the plot on the back cover
   - ☐ book review I read
   - ☐ other _____

(Continued...)

6. Please list your three favorite contemporary romance lines.
   _____
   _____

7. Please list your favorite authors of contemporary romance lines.
   _____
   _____
   _____
   _____
   _____

8. How many SECOND CHANCE AT LOVE romances have you read? _____

9. How many series romances like SECOND CHANCE AT LOVE do you <u>read</u> each month? _____

10. How many series romances like SECOND CHANCE AT LOVE do you <u>buy</u> each month? _____

11. Mind telling your age?
    ☐ under 18
    ☐ 18 to 30
    ☐ 31 to 45
    ☐ over 45

☐ Please check if you'd like to receive our <u>free</u> SECOND CHANCE AT LOVE Newsletter.

We hope you'll share your other ideas about romances with us on an additional sheet and attach it securely to this questionnaire.

• •

Fill in your name and address below:
Name _____
Street Address _____
City _____ State _____ Zip _____

Please return this questionnaire to:
   SECOND CHANCE AT LOVE
   The Berkley Publishing Group
   200 Madison Avenue, New York, New York 10016